PROTÉGÉ OF A LEGEND 2

Corey Robinson

**Lock Down Publications and Ca$h
Presents**

Protégé of a Legend 2
A Novel by *Corey Robinson*

Corey Robinson

Lock Down Publications
Po Box 944
Stockbridge, Ga 30281

Visit our website @
www.lockdownpublications.com

Copyright 2023 by Corey Robinson
Protégé of a Legend 2

Lock Down Publications
Like our page on Facebook: Lock Down Publications @
www.facebook.com/lockdownpublications.ldp
Book interior design by: **Shawn Walker**

Stay Connected with Us!

Text **LOCKDOWN** to 22828 to stay up-to-date with new releases, sneak peaks, contests and more…
Thank you.

Corey Robinson

Submission Guideline.

Submit the first three chapters of your completed manuscript to ldpsubmissions@gmail.com, subject line: Your book's title. The manuscript must be in a .doc file and sent as an attachment. Document should be in Times New Roman, double spaced and in size 12 font. Also, provide your synopsis and full contact information. If sending multiple submissions, they must each be in a separate email.

Have a story but no way to send it electronically? You can still submit to LDP/Ca$h Presents. Send in the first three chapters, written or typed, of your completed manuscript to:

LDP: Submissions Dept
Po Box 944
Stockbridge, Ga 30281

DO NOT send original manuscript. Must be a duplicate.

Provide your synopsis and a cover letter containing your full contact information.

Thanks for considering LDP and Ca$h Presents.

Protégé of a Legend 2

FOR CA$H
THE REAL LEGEND

7

Corey Robinson

Prologue
Krystal

Every time I made the trip to Baltimore, I told myself that it would be the last one but I knew it was a lie. I enjoyed getting away from everything but were the chances I was taking even worth it? Brandon tried to convince me to leave Marcus every time I went but I felt like I still owed him for saving my life all those months ago plus my love for him was deep.

Marcus' visits to see me had gotten less frequent and I knew in my gut that he had someone else taking my place. I tried and tried to get him to admit it but what man in their right mind would? Brandon suggested that I start pocketing money and stashing it just in case I came across an emergency but I would never take anything from Marcus without him knowing it. I wasn't that kind of person.

When I got back to town, I decided not to go back to where Marcus had moved me to. Instead, I went back to the place we once shared and when I didn't see his vehicle there, I let myself in. I walked all over the house just to see if I could find traces of another woman and it eased my heart when I didn't. However, I still had that feeling in my gut.

I went into the bedroom and ran my small hands over the bed we used to share. The covers were still as soft as before, the same ones that covered a man with a hardened heart. I pulled out the drawer of the bedside table and saw the gun. I hurriedly shut it but opened it right back up, I pulled the gun out and sat there in deep thought for a minute before putting the weapon in my purse.

I finally got up and went back out to go to another mission. My determination had me breathing heavy and made me drive around all the streets of the city until I saw it. There it was, parked in front of a room, but I needed to make sure before I went in, so I listened.

I suddenly had a change of mind and decided to walk away but a voice caused me to turn back. That was my moment and I couldn't let it slip away. I refused to. I had come too far to turn back now. My small hand gripped the door knob and was shocked to find it unlocked. I turned it and pushed the door open in hopes of finding what I'd been looking for.

Chapter One
FELLOW

My Glock was loaded and ready for action and I wasn't beyond shooting anybody that moved wrong and got in my way. "That bitch gonna eat one of these bullets when I find her ass," I said out loud to myself as my feet shuffled across the trash-strewn streets.

I had made it halfway down the alley when I heard a voice call my name from a dimly lit corner. "Fee! Yo, Fee, man. Let me hold a little something till Friday," the fiend stated through dry cracked lips. I looked into the crackhead's bulging eyes and almost felt bad for him but the hate and anger in my heart overrode any ounce of compassion I'd ever had. "Nigga, suck, my muthafucking dick. I ain't giving yo' ass shit," I said with bass in my voice. The crackhead instantly dropped to his knees in front of me to perform the task I had just given him. When he did, he found himself staring into the barrel of my gun. I asked him, "Where the fuck that bitch Keisha at?" The crackhead trembled in fear but answered my question anyway," Man Fee. I-I-I don't know man. She ain't been around in a minute but word on the street is that she with yo' boss!"

The thought of Keisha being with Marcus made me smile because maybe things could still turn out as planned. I knew that I needed to find her and make things right. I also knew that I needed to make things right with Marcus so that he would trust me again. We were once like brothers but somewhere along the way, I had lost all respect for him. I swore that it was him that made Ditto call me and try to get me to switch over to his crew. I felt like he had tested my loyalty to him and my heart was crushed. I had never been anything but loyal to Marcus and actually missed my brother but I somehow felt that things would never be the same between us again.

I lowered my gun and said to the fiend who was still on his knees in front of me. "If you see that bitch around here, you call me immediately." I paused and gave him my number and a small baggie full of rocks and then said,

"You'll be rewarded greatly for that call." The fiend looked at the baggie and licked his dry lips and said. "I got you Fee. I-I-I got you. I'll call you as soon as I see her. I give you my word." He then got up off his knees and ran back to the dimly lit corner he'd come from.

I turned around and walked back down the alley. Once I reached my truck. I got in and shut the door and reminisced about the times Marcus and I had shared growing up, the times before Marcus was introduced to the dope game by Ditto. I was jarred out of my thoughts by the vibration of my cell phone. I pulled it out of my pocket and without checking to see who the caller was, I answered, "Yeah, what's good?" The voice that came from the other end made my heart beat faster than ever before.

"Fee man, we need to talk. Let's meet up. Some shit gonna have to change my nigga." Marcus said into the phone as I listened.

I chose my words wisely and stated, "Name the time and place and I'll be there."

"The park where we used to play ball at when we were kids. Two hours. And Fee, don't bring no weapon. We gotta put this shit to rest."

When I heard the dial tone, I held the phone for a minute and then finally hung up. My mind wondered what would happen if I really went to that park without my piece, but I wouldn't take that chance and find out.

****

MARCUS

I was ready to end the beef with Fee once and for all. We had come up together and had been best friends all our lives, so there should have never been any kind of division between us. I had forgiven anything he had ever done against me because he was like my own blood. There were bigger things for us to worry about in the streets without us bringing more drama to the crew. Ditto and Echo were still out there and one of them if not both had slowly knocked some of my men down. I needed Fee to get his shit together so we could beat them niggas at their own game. The streets belonged to us and we were a team. I had other niggas on my squad but I wanted my main man back beside me where he belonged because together, we were a force to be reckoned with.

The warm hand that gripped my dick pulled me from my thoughts. I looked over at the bitch I had in the bed beside me and said, "You gripping that muthafucka like you know what to do with it. Come on and show a nigga what you working with." The bitch then dropped her head and replaced her hand with her warm wet mouth. The suction caused me to lean my head back and moan in pleasure. "Mmm Hmm, ah shit. yeah, do it just like that"

I had sent Krystal on another run to Baltimore and knew that she wouldn't be back to the house for awhile. My dick couldn't wait any longer, so I picked up a bitch I had met only days ago and took her to the motel. I figured I could get some pussy, meet up with Feelow and then be at the crib I had moved Krystal to, all before she made it back to town.

Krystal had ended up being a real rider for a nigga and I kept her tucked away for her own safety because the life I lived wasn't the place for a white girl. I knew that she wasn't the average female, so I had to do things a little differently. I also knew that I felt something for her, I just couldn't place my hand on exactly what it was.

However, I used the feelings she had for me against her just to make her stronger. I didn't need a bitch to bow down to my ass but I damn sure needed one to bow down to my dick like the one in front of me had done. I looked at my watch and saw that I had plenty of time to bust a nut and then I turned the bitch over on all fours.

****

ECHO

"Yo, Echo how long do you expect me to sit back and let shit go?" Toe Tag asked me with a murderous look in his eyes. I knew

13

he was ready to kill all of Marcus' men until he went to the man himself but I knew careless moving could only get us knocked off.

Swag T cut in. " Damn, nigga, that bitch dead and gone and you still strung the fuck out. Bitch must have sucked the hair off yo asshole or something. Damn."

"Bitch, fuck you. Don't you need to change your tampon or something?" Toe Tag snapped back and as always I had to be the peacemaker.

"Yo, y'all bitches chill the fuck out. We gon get that ass when the time is right. I'm waiting on something to come through and then we gon' get that nigga popped along with anyone who stands in our way." I looked both of them in the eyes and shook my head and right before I opened my mouth again, my cell rang. I looked at the caller information and then answered, "Damn nigga, what the fuck took you so long to call?" I listened while the voice on the other end spoke back to me.

"Man I needed to make sure that shit was right. I can't afford to raise no more suspicion right now but everything is falling into place"

I then asked, "So, when can I make this shit pop off? I done sat long enough." I paused and looked up at Toe Tag and then to Swag and said, "My niggas, trigger fingers is ready to clap that ass and I don't think he has much more patience left."

"Tell them niggas to chill and give me a couple of more days. I got a meeting to go to and then I'll get back at you on the move," he stated matter of factly.

I let out a short sigh and said, "Two more days nigga, and then we move without you."

****

KRYSTAL

"Pull out bitch."

I had finally caught him red-handed and balls deep in some pussy that wasn't mine. I had felt for the longest that Marcus had been dipping but could never prove it. Like all the other men in the

14

world, he would deny it to the bitter end. I just couldn't understand why he would want anyone else. I fucked him real good and sucked his dick until he came down my throat, so there was just no excuse.

"Baby, it's not what it looks like," Marcus lied, with a little fear in his voice and his hand held out in front of him. I knew that he would feed me lies and bullshit but what exactly could he say to justify fucking another bitch?

The female suddenly tried to grab her clothes but I wasn't having that shit. "Nah bitch, don't get your ugly ass dressed now." I stared angrily with tears in my eyes that had threatened to fall at any given moment. The bitch had the game fucked up if she thought that I was just gonna let her go without any repercussions. She had chosen the wrong dick to jump on today and I had planned to make her pay dearly for it.

I stood over my nigga and that beat-down ass hoe and pointed a gun that I didn't even know how to shoot. However, neither of them knew that, so I was going to play it out until I got my point across. I was tired of being used and lied to and wouldn't put that gun down until Marcus understood my message.

"I should put a bullet in your fucking skull," I said while I looked deep into his eyes. The bitch whimpered and I knew she wondered if I was really going to pull the trigger but little did she know, his ass wasn't even worth the bullet that I had taken out and left in the drawer at home.

"Krystal, baby come on. Put the gun down. I'll do whatever you need me to do, just put that shit down." Marcus pleaded but his words didn't mean shit to me anymore. I should have listened to Brandon and dipped on his ass but my heart stood in the way. I caught the bitch moving again from the corner of my eye and when she did I reacted by hitting her with the butt of the gun. "Move again bitch and the next time, you'll be sucking on this barrel instead of my man's dick."

I looked back to Marcus and as a tear finally escaped, I said to him. "I've been nothing but loyal to you. I've risked my life and my freedom for your black ass and this is what you spend your time doing while I'm out there taking chances so you don't have to. Huh? You disrespectful muthafucker."

Marcus stood from the edge of the bed and reached out for me but I wouldn't let shit go that easy. I pushed the gun against his bare chest and shouted," Sit the fuck back down Marcus" He held both of his hands up but remained standing and asked me again. "What can I do to make this up to you? I'll do anything to make it right." I stared at him and thought about his question and then stated in a stern voice" Put me all the way in." Marcus looked at me like I'd lost my mind and asked, "Fuck you mean?"

"I mean just what I said." I exclaimed a little more demandingly, "Put me all the way in or I will find someone who will."

****

MARCUS

I had to give it to her, that white bitch had some muthfuckin' nerve to ask me to put her all the way in my operation. The only thing that persuaded me was the gun she had pointed at my chest. I wasn't sure if she was capable of shooting me but my black ass wasn't willing to take that chance and find out. I knew when I saw her ass going down that alley that she had potential but never expected her to use it against me but I guess you can never put anything past a woman scorned.

"Aiight, I'll put you all the way in but yo' ass better not act all prissy and shit, like a real fucking white girl," I said to her in a serious yet, playful tone. The room was quiet for a second and I looked from her to the bitch she caught me with and said.

"You know you could lower that gun from in front of me now. I got the point and you got what you wanted. "I lifted my hand and put it over the gun and pulled it gently from her grasp and then stepped up closer to her and said. "Damn, girl, that gangsta shit done turned a nigga on, What's up?"

She looked down and saw that my dick was hard again and lifted an eyebrow before she said. "That shit is not going anywhere near me until it is washed. I don't know where this bitch has been but as a matter of fact," she turned her head towards the naked bitch and stated in a demanding voice that only a boss would use. "Bitch, why the fuck are you even still here?" Get your shit and get your ass out and if I ever see you near my man again, I'm shooting for real."

The girl jumped up and grabbed her clothes but didn't bother to even put them on. Instead, she ran out of the room butt-ass naked. Me and Krystal looked at each other and laughed. No sooner than the room door shut, my cell began to buzz. I looked and saw that it was Feelow. "Oh shit, I forgot" I stated frantically right before I answered. "Yo, my nigga I apologize but I was caught up in some real live shit. I'm at the mo six on Fairfield, room one fourteen. Why don't you swing through here instead?"

"Damn Dawg, that shits way across town but I'll be there in a few, and Marcus, you better not be bringing me in with no bullshit." Feelow stated and then hung up.

There used to be a time in our lives when we didn't question each other's motives and I hated that the shit between us had come to this. I looked at my girl and then my watch and said, "That was my nigga. He gon' be coming through but we got time to hop in the shower and get one in real quick if you down." She looked down at my dick one more time and smiled, then she stated hungrily, "Hmm, I'm always down for some of that."

Corey Robinson

Chapter Two
DITTO

"I think you should just let it go and move on. Maybe start fresh and rebuild" The woman lying beside me said. I turned my head and looked at her like she'd lost her damn mind and exclaimed, "Bitch, what the fuck are you saying? I taught that little bastard everything he knows about the game. That muthfucka owes me and I'm ready to collect. What the fuck are you talking 'bout? Let some shit go. I've lost everything because of his fuck ass and have no clue of how I'm gonna rebuild."

I sat up on the side of the bed and planted my feet on the floor with attitude. I suddenly felt her come up behind me and when she wrapped her arms around me, it pissed me off even more. I grabbed her by the wrists and puller her arms off of me. I stood up and faced her and said angrily, "What do you think? Some pussy gon' make me soft and shit? Bitch, you pass that shit around like bowls in a soup kitchen. That nigga is where he's at because of me and yo' ass think I'm supposed to sit down and let it be. Your pussy ain't that damn good. I can still focus!"

She smacked her lips like she had a real reason to be mad but what I had going on didn't have shit to do with her. I just wanted her to listen; I didn't expect any feedback. I was there with her to bust a nut, not for her to tell me what to do when it came to my street affairs. However, her next words threw me off even more.

"Well, my cousin Heather works for a nigga named Stanley Earl. He is singing and shit in the clubs trying to get noticed so he can get into the music business but his real black ass don't know how to do nothing but pimp hoes." She stopped talking for a minute as if she had to gather her thoughts. I wondered why she had given me that information, so I asked. "Why in the fuck would. I care about a nigga named Stanley Earl? Bitch, how is that shit relevant to what I'm going through. I need a new connection, not some pimp to serenade my ass."

She smacked her lips and let out a small laugh before she said, "Nah, dummy. Stanley Earl supplies the suppliers. He's the boss of all bosses and I might just be able to hook you up with him." I smiled at the thought of getting back in the game but this time, I would play it like a ghost in the night. I sat back down on the bed and pulled Sarah into me and thought that it might be smart to keep her around for a while.

****

KEISHA

It had been a minute since I had gotten high and I was about to lose my mind from being shut inside all the time but Marcus thought that it would be best for me and the baby I carried. My belly was getting big and every time I felt a little punch in my gut, I thought of Feelow. "Damn, I miss that nigga," I said out loud. Although I knew that no one else could hear me, deep down I wished that someone could.

I was so lonely and the only company I'd had was Marcus when he would drop by to bring me food or other things I'd needed. He had been a complete gentleman and I was shocked that the hadn't tried to fuck me. My mind told me that I'd become less attractive since getting pregnant but Marcus assured me that I was finer than ever before and that he was just trying to respect Feelow although they were on the outs. "That could be my little niece or nephew in there. I mean, no matter what, that nigga is still my brother," Marcus would say. I looked at my phone where it sat on the table in front of me and wondered if Feelow still had the same number. I was itching to call him and thought that maybe I could just dial his number and hear his voice and then I would hang up. I wondered if he'd know it was me. I bit my bottom lip as I picked up the phone. When the phone rang in my hand, I drew blood.

****

TOE TAG

"Echo who the fuck was that?' I asked once he pulled the phone from his ear. "That was Feelow. He 'bout to meet up with someone and then he's gonna get back with us about the hit on Marcus," he said with a puzzled look on his face. Somehow, I felt like Echo knew that Feelow was lying. Shit just wasn't adding up and I knew that Toe Tag was tired of sitting around waiting to avenge Carla's death.

Toe Tag exclaimed, "A meeting? That muthafucka 'bout to have a meeting with one of these bullets along with his partner. Nigga up to some shit if you ask me."

"Yeah Tag, I'm feeling the same vibe. I think we should move without him." I said and then looked at Echo and stated, "Yo' man, you ain't never waited on another nigga to move. Fuck is up with that?" Echo looked at me through black soulless eyes and said, "Bitch why the fuck do you question my moves? Marcus is young, but he ain't no dumb ass nigga. He knows people are out to get him. Not only us but that nigga Ditto still out there lurking somewhere so his bitch ass is cautions."

Toe Tag cut in, "Man, I'm with swag on this cause; I'm tired of waiting and with or without your word, I'm doing what needs to be done and I'm doing it soon. That nigga killed my bitch and you expect me to sit around and not avenge her. Nigga, you got me fucked up." Toe Tag stood up to leave the room and I laughed and said, "Man Carla was the communities' bitch and everybody knows that you can't turn a hoe into a housewife."

"Bitch why don't you go and suck a dick with your wanna be a man ass. Carla was mine and I know I could have changed her but that muthafucka took that away from me and if either of you gets in my way, you can join his ass" Toe Tag hollered and then walked out and slammed the door behind him.

****

PARIS

There had been no sign of Ditto since Torrie's death but I knew that he was out there somewhere. I could feel his presence. That nigga was like a stray cat with nine lives but if I ever got a hold of him, I would take them all. My pop's voice broke me from my thoughts "What's on your mind son?" You look like you're far away."

I looked up at him and said, "I'm just thinking about Torrie and the baby. I ain't gonna be able to let them rest until that nigga pays for his violation. She was the love of my fuckin' life pops and she ain't did shit to nobody. I ain't even get to see my seed take a breath. I'll never even know if he would have looked like me or her. That muthafucka owes me and I'm ready to collect."

"Paris, son. I need you to think with a level head right now. I know your heart is broken but if you try to jump too quickly, you could lose your opportunity," he said when he sat at the table in front of me. I wasn't trying to listen to shit he had to say, though. I looked up at him with murder in my eyes and said, "Fuck what you talkin' 'bout. I'm going to find that muthafucka if he doesn't surface soon and I'm killing anything that gets in my way, so I suggest you stay back if you don't wanna feel this wrath!"

I stood to walk out of the room but he stood up in front of me and hollered in, my face while spit spewed from his mouth, "Yo ass wanna challenge me? Huh? Muthafucka I made yo' ass and you gonna fucking listen to me whether you want to or not. I went through this same shit when that bastard took your mother from me so I know how it feels" I saw tears in his eyes and he shut them for a brief second to keep them at bay and then said in a calmer voice, "Son, we all we got, and we have to do this right or we could both lose our lives going against him. I want his ass just as bad as you but I need you to fall back and trust me. I got you, son. I got you."

I stood there in a challenging stance and listened to what he did. I knew in my mind that he was right but my heart had no understanding. My pulse quickened at the thought of holding a child that I would never meet and I could feel the wetness form in my eyes. I tried my best to hold it in but–as soon as the first teardrop fell my, pops pulled me into him and said. "Push' em out son. The same way you're going to push them bullets out on that nigga. I promise you, we gon' get him."

****

FEELOW

"So you just gon' keep avoiding a nigga and shit?" I asked as soon as Keisha answered the phone.

"How did you even get this number Feelow?" She asked me in a low nervous tone.

"When a nigga wants to find shit out bad enough, all he has to do is go to the right places. Where's your ass at with my seed Keisha?" I replied. Had been thinking a lot about the baby she carried. At first, I denied that it was mine but I knew deep down that once I gave Keisha the dick, she had not let anyone else dip in my zone. Her response felt like a hard punch in the gut. "I aborted the little bastard and if I remember correctly, you said it wasn't yours, so why the fuck do you care?"

"Yeah, you're right. I did deny it but that didn't mean for your ass to go and kill it. Damn, I just needed to clear my head and do some thinking. Fuck, Keisha. A nigga had a lot of shit going on but I knew it was mine. Bitch, when I find you, I'm gonna beat that ass about my seed." I said with hurt in my voice, but her reply healed quickly.

"Nah nigga, I'm lying. Damn, do you really think that I could be that cruel? I could never kill my baby. I was hurt when you denied him but not enough for me to harm him," she stated in a sincere voice.

"Wait a minute. You keep saying to *him*. Does that mean?" I asked curiously but she cut me off before I could finish my question.

"Yes, Feelow, I said *him*, we are having a son and that little nigga is hot-headed. Just like his damn daddy. His lil' ass is kicking the hell outta me. I think he is sending me signals telling me he wants to meet you but he has a little more cooking to do before he comes outta this oven" she said while she laughed which brought a smile to my face. I couldn't believe that I had a son coming and couldn't wait to groom him into a little soldier.

I asked. "Yo Keisha, when can I see you? I wanna rub that belly and maybe even talk to my boy. Ya know, I think it would be good to let him hear my voice. So what's up?"

"I don't know Feelow. Yo ass is tripping and shit plus if you still on that pipe, I can't be around you. I don't want to be around anyone or anything that could make me slip and relapse on that shit. I ain't trying to have no crack baby." I felt the seriousness in her voice.

I responded "You damn right you ain't gon have no crack baby. I got you Keisha. I would never do that shit around my kid whether he's been born or not. But damn Boo, can a nigga get some of that wet?"

She laughed at my question and asked. "Where can we meet?"

****

STANLEY EARL

I heard when her phone rang and said. "Uh uh. Don't answer that shit. Yo' ass needs to finish me off first."

No sooner than I'd said it she lifted her head and said, "I have to, Stanley Earl. It could be something important."

"Important? Bitch ain't nothing more important right now than this dick. Come on. I'm almost there" My plea didn't work because she answered the phone anyway. I stood up and then pulled my boxers up and when I started to walk away, I heard her say "Stanley Earl, it's for you."

I looked at the bitch like she was crazy and asked. "What the fuck do you mean it's for me? Why the fuck would someone be calling your phone looking for me?"

She smiled an innocent smile and said as seductively as she could "cause they know that no matter what, I'm your rider. Come on, it's my cousin Sarah." Heather had been my bottom bitch from day one and she had proven her loyalty. When I first met her, I was singing in clubs trying to make ends meet and hoping to get noticed. I had always wanted to break into the music business but when she told me she had some girls that would be willing to sell their pussy and lace my pockets, I jumped on it. All they wanted in return was for me to keep them safe and to take care of them too. That shit sounded too sweet to pass up and the thought of always having pussy on stand-by made it even better."

Sarah replied "Stanley Earl, I got a nigga here who wants to meet up with you. He's interested in buying a set of encyclopedias from you and his money is right."

I was a little pissed at Sarah for calling me about a nigga that she had most likely just met. Sarah was Heather's cousin who had hooked me up with a lot of low-level street dealers but it had always been niggas I'd heard of and knew that their street cred was legit. However, Sarah was smart and I knew that she had to have done her homework on the dude before calling me, so I gave her the benefit of the doubt and stated. "Aiight.

Let me get a hold of Thomas and I'll hit you back."

"Thanks Stanley, I'll be waiting for your call," she said sweetly and right before she hung up I asked, "Yo Sarah, what's this niggas name?"

She replied, "His name is Dittrick but the streets call him Ditto.

Corey Robinson

Chapter Three
KRYSTAL

It felt as if the walls would close in on me. I heard the women shout at me as if I'd done something wrong to them. I'd been there for months and yet, I'd heard nothing from Marcus. I didn't understand why he didn't reach out to me. I had done everything for him and it was as if I no longer existed.

I wondered what he had been doing and most of all, who he had been doing it with. I was lonely and heartbroken and mostly stayed to myself. I didn't want anyone around me to be nosey and ask questions because I would never let them use Marcus to help their own cases.

I was bred by a legend and knew how to keep my mouth shut. I would die before I would betray Marcus and I was determined to do the time like a soldier because that's what a Boss Bitch would do. I figured that Marcus was just waiting for things to die down and then he would send me a letter and perhaps, even come visit. There's no way he would just let me sit in prison for a crime he committed and not ride with me. Marcus would come around. I just knew it.

****
MARCUS

BOOM…..BOOM……BOOM…..BOOM……BOOM……BOOM….BOOM

The loud banging on the door made me jump but I instantly knew who it was. Me and Feelow had a coded knock that we had made up when we were kids. I would use the knock at his window on the nights that I had to get away from my mother's bullshit.

"Who the fuck is that?" Krystal asked and jumped up in a paranoid stance. I laughed at her and said, "Girl, just chill. That is my nigga at the door." I went and opened the door and as soon as I saw him, I pulled him in for a brotherly hug. I had missed my boy and wanted him back by my side. "Yo, Fee man. It's so good to see you! Come on in Dawg. We got a lot to talk about."

Fee smiled back at me but he hesitated when he walked in and saw Krystal.

"Man, we gon do this shit with her here? Are you fuckin crazy?" He asked while he looked from me to her.

I said, "I want her here. I'm pulling her into the operation. I think she could bring a lot to our organization. She's ready and I'm confident that she gon' ride for a nigga. Plus, mutha fuckas will never see it coming."

"Hell no. Have you lost yo' damn mind? The last thing we need is a bitch on the team. You know that females are known to fall weak in times of desperation. Fuckin everybody knows that. What the fuck are you thinking man? You gon ' get our black asses cased the fuck up." Feelow said and then turned around to leave. As soon as he grabbed the door handle, Krystal spoke. "I ain't a soft or a weak bitch. Just give me a chance. I can handle this shit just as good as a man can."

Feelow let the door handle go and looked at me before he shook his head. I raised an eyebrow and said, "Trust me man. You already know that if she doesn't turn out right, I'll kill her ass myself. But I'm telling you man, she's ready for this hit." Feelow let out a loud sigh and then said, "Nah bro, if she fucks up, I'm going to kill the bitch."

****

TRAP

"Yo', man, the streets are mighty quiet. I feel like some shit bout to go down," I said to a Creep while he sat back and watched the Cleveland Browns beat the Tampa Bay Buccaneers. Creep finally cut his eyes from the television and said "Yeah, dawg, shit been quiet. Money has been coming in like a muthafucka and the five-o ain't even been creeping. That shit crazy."

I got up and went to look out the window. I felt in my gut that the war with Ditto was far from over and knew that he was still out there lurking somewhere although no one had seen or heard from him. A muthafucka like Ditto didn't go away that easily. I wondered when he would surface because I knew that eventually he would and when he did, all hell would break loose.

"Ah fuck," I said and quickly let the blinds go. Creep jumped up from his chair and pulled out his burner and asked "Man, what the fuck is going on out there?" I put a finger to my lips to silence him. A second later, a knock came at the door along with the shouting, "Open up this damn door Crestin. I know your ass in there and I'm not leaving until I see your black ass." Carrie McDonald was Creep's ex-girlfriend, and a crazy ass white bitch, she hadn't been around in a while and when I heard she was back in town, I knew that she would eventually show up. Creep gave her the first piece of dark meant she'd ever had and that bitch had been off the chain ever since.

"Man, what the fuck am I gonna do? Damn, I didn't think I'd ever see that bitch again. Shit, shit, shit," Creep said while he hunched down by the wall. I gave him the only advice I could think of. I said "Man, I think you should answer the door before that crazy bitch gets the wrong people's attention. You already know she ain't leaving until she gets what she came for."

"Hell no. I am not sticking my dick, back up in the crazy bitch. You see what it's done to her. Uh Uh man. You fuck that bitch because my black ass is outta here," Creep stated in a serious tone and then walked out of the room. I knew that he'd gone down to our hidden room that we had in case of an emergency so he could get away from her.

"Damn it, I'ma kill that muthafucka as soon as I get rid of this bitch," I said out loud to myself and then I went to open the door.

As soon as I had the lock unsecured, Carrie burst through the door and yelled, "Where is Crestins black ass at? I know he's in here. Crestin, Crestin. I know he's in here, so come on out" I tried to calm her down and said in a soothing voice, "Yo Carrie, you too damn pretty to be acting like that! Why are you tripping on my boy and shit?"

"Compliments are not going to calm me down Travis. The last time I saw Crestin, he said that he was gonna call me and I've been patient for months but dammit, I don't have any patience left. I'm not going to allow him to treat me like those jump-offs he runs up in. Hell no, that shit is not gonna happen" She said and continued to look around and then added, "I know he's here because his car is outside, so don't stand there and play me like a dumb bitch. You already know that my ass will start swinging."

She walked through the house going room to room until she finally gave up. Carrie looked at me and let out a short sigh. "Well, I guess I'll just sit here and wait for him then."

When she sat on the couch, I knew that I was in for a long night.

****

MARCUS

I knew him better than I knew myself, so the gun he had concealed came as no surprise. However, it told me that we had a lot more building to get back right. I asked, "Yo man, what's up with the burner? I asked you to leave it behind, so why are you tripping?" I had told Krystal to watch my back, so if he moved wrong, I trusted her to handle that. I Just hoped the bitch really knew how to handle a gun.

"Hey, we have been through a lot of shit, so it ain't like I don't trust you. It's just more of a habit than anything else. I'm gon' take the ammo out and sit it right here on the table but I think we should step outside to talk," Feelow said and then emptied his clip.

I followed Feelow outside and once the door was shut behind us, he began to speak, "Marcus my brother, I'm gon' apologize for the doubts I held. Man, I know you ain't never did shit against me but my fuckin' paranoia wouldn't subside." He pulled in a long breath and gripped the railing in front of him. I started saying something in response but he cut me off, "I just want us to be back like we were man. That's all. I miss those days and I know this shit is all my fault but if you'll forgive me, nigga, I'll never slip again. You, my family and you all I got."

I replied sincerely "I have forgiven you Fee. I ain't gon' lie though, that shit did something to a niggas heart. Man, I'll kill a muthafuck over you and I've had men killed for less than what you did to me but shit ain't right on the team without you. I just wanna put this shit behind us and get back on track like we were."

He smiled and when I held out my hand, he took it in his and then pulled me in for a brotherly hug and said, "Nigga, let's get out there and take our shit back. This is our fuckin city and them bastards can either get down with us or get laid down for going against us."

"That's my nigga talking right there, welcome home, bro," I stated with a voice full of joy. Feelow had done a lot of shit against me but I couldn't give up on him just yet; we had been a team since we were kids and without him, it felt like a piece of me was a missing. As the night sent a cool breeze our way, I stated, "Let's get out here and sit them other niggas down.

****

CREEP

I didn't know what was going on upstairs but I was certain that Trap would alert me when Carrie was gone. Carrie was the first and last white girl I had been with. At first, she seemed to be a lot of fun to hang around and never tripped when I sent bullshit her way. She was selfish with the pussy at first but she eventually gave up the goods and once I slid the dick to her, she seemed to lose her damn mind. One day she had caught me with another bitch and left the crib without saying a word. I thought shit was sweet until I heard the dogs barking. I got up from beside the bitch I had in my bed and went to look out the window only to see Carrie's pretty ass standing in the middle of two large mastiffs. When she noticed me peeking, she hollered out," I see you Crestin and you got thirty seconds to put that bitch out the door or I'm sending Heyman and Karma in to get her. It's your choice."

I had to give it to her, that white bitch was bold and as I thought back to that incident, I got a little turned on. I smiled to myself and decided to take my black ass upstairs and face the only bitch that really gave a fuck about me.

****

STANLEY EARL

When I picked up my boy Thomas, I decided to ask him if he had ever heard of the nigga Sarah had with her. "Yo, Thomas man, you ever hear of a nigga that the streets call Ditto?" He looked at me but held his words for a second as if he had to think about it.

He turned his head to look back out the window and then answered my question, "Yeah Stan, I only heard of one Ditto but I don't know if it's the same cat. What all did she say about him?"

I replied, "She said he use to be big-time but some lil nigga under him decided to break off from the pack and do his own thing which put him into a fucked up position. The nigga had a hit out on his life so he's been hanging low for a minute until shit dies down but now he is supposed to be ready to move again."

Thomas nodded his head. "I bet this is the same nigga because his ass has been a ghost for a while. If it is, he 'bout that money but his ass is grimey as fuck too. He's an older G, so he does his dirt the old, fashioned way. However, I ain't met a nigga yet that can pull one over on me without getting caught so if he ain't right, I'm a push his wig back."

I shared a laugh with my right hand and turned into the complex that Sarah lived in. Before we got out of the car, I asked Thomas, "Yo', you got that gat ready just in case?"

Thomas pulled out his nine and put one in the chamber and said, "Nigga, me and my bitch stay ready."

****

PARIS

"You right Pops. I'm a chill out. I just want his ass so bad, it makes my fuckin dick hard," I said but knew in my mind that I was lying. There was no way I could sit back and wait on my father to help me find Ditto and kill him. He had waited years before he made the move to avenge my mother's death. And I just couldn't let it go for that long. However, I would listen to his plan and his reason just to appease him but I was murking Ditto with or without his ass.

He patted me on the shoulder. "That's good son. I'm glad that you've decided to listen to me because I know that muthafucka as well as I know myself. You just gotta trust me on this."

"I do trust you but damn how long is that bastard gonna stay under? Pops, it's been months and fuck boy ain't resurfaced," I stated in an agitated tone.

He responded with the same words he'd been saying for months, "Don't worry, he'll show his face again. He's not the type of man who stays hidden because he likes to be on the scene and run shit. However, he needs his crew to help him but he knows all of them have switched over with Marcus' team, so he's gonna have to come out and rebuild. When he does, that's when we will shoot him down."

I was silent while I thought for a minute and then suddenly I remembered and stated, "Nah pops, you're wrong. All of his men didn't switch over. One of them just was chilling and waiting for his return. They act like he is down for us but the muthafucka was waiting on his word." He looked at me confused and asked, "What are you saying Paris? I was there at the meeting when everyone took a truce and agreed to all be on the same team."

I looked him in the eyes with a serious expression and said, "Yeah, I was there too but I didn't see Blackout agree to shit. He was always the most loyal to that nigga and the most feared of the crew. That nigga has been chilling with everyone but all it will take is one call from D and his ass will start dropping muthafukcas. He will play along for now, though."

"Aiight then son," He said before he pulled out his burner and cocked a bullet in the chamber and when he looked back at me, I knew what he was going to say before he said it, "Well, let's go pay a visit to Blackout and show him that we can play along too."

****

KEISHA

The call from Feelow had me excited and anxious to be close to him. The baby inside of me seemed to be excited too because he had kicked the hell out of me ever since our call ended. I sat and waited hoping that his next call would come soon. It felt like forever had passed before the phone finally rang again. "You ready for some of this wet pussy, nigga?" I asked in a seductive voice while my heart sped up and waited for his response. However, it wasn't the person I'd been waiting for.

"Yo', what the fuck, Keisha?" Marcus yelled into the phone.

"Oh my god! Marcus, I am so sorry. I thought…I thought."

"You thought what! Huh? Yo, who the fuck have you been talking to?" he asked angrily.

"I'm sorry Marcus. I should have probably called and told you but Feelow called me earlier. He wants to meet up and make amends. He was so happy about the baby and wants us to be a family," I stated nervously and hoped that Marcus would be okay with what I'd just revealed.

"How in the fuck did he get the new number?" Marcus asked. "Who the fuck have you called since I put you up in that place Keisha? And you better tell me the fuckin truth or I'm a put your ass out."

"I've only talked to my cousin Tammy and I swear I didn't tell her where I was. Shit Marcus, I'm fucking lonely here and I'm about to lose my damn mind. I needed to talk to someone and besides, I ain't never gone this long without some dick" I stated with attitude.

Marcus said, "Shit, look, Keisha, I just met up with Fee and he is talking right but I'm not sure it's a good idea for you to see him yet. Let me make sure this nigga is being for real and if he is, I'll set something up."

"Damn nigga, are we making this move or not?" I heard Feelow holler out at Marcus. I froze, while wondering if Feelow knew that it was me Marcus was talking to.

I asked, "Does he know you're talking to me?"

"Nah. He doesn't know shit and that's how we gon keep it for now. Let me feel this nigga out. I give you my word, If he ain't still on that fucking shit, I'll set it up. Just chill for now. I'm just trying to keep you and my nephew safe" Marcus whispered.

I smacked my lips and said, "Okay, Marcus, I won't answer the phone anymore without making sure it's you. I promise, "I only hoped that he believed the lie I just told him."

****

FEELOW

Somehow, I knew that it was Keisha on the other end of that conversation Marcus had on the phone. Marcus had always talked in front of me and even though we had not been right in a minute, I felt like he still trusted me. I wasn't sure why he felt the need to hide Keisha out but it wasn't hard for me to find someone who would give me Keisha's new number. After the crackhead had told me he'd heard she was with Marcus, I knew exactly what I needed to do.

Her cousin Tammy had been on my nut sack for years, so when I ran across her one day, I'd given her what she'd been craving. While I fucked her long and hard, I asked her if she'd heard from Keisha and the dick had her singling like a bird. Even though she didn't know Keisha's location, the number would get me close enough. Eventually, the rest would fall into place.

No matter how much shit I talked, I would never harm my seed. I got lost in thought and wondered if my son would be like me when he grew up. Would he be bisexual like his pops? Would he smoke crack and turn against his boy like I did or would he be a loyal muthafucka? Would I even be around to raise him or would my lifestyle prevent that? All I knew was that I would make sure he was a soldier.

The knock on the window cut my thoughts short. "Yo, man, you aiight in there?" Marcus asked. I wanted to spit on that muthafucka but now isn't the time, so I played nice instead. "Yeah, yeah. I was just. I was just thinking about some shit. Yo, who were you just talking to?"

He said, "Ah man, that wasn't nobody important. Just a bitch I gotta meet up with later, that's all." When I didn't respond, he added, "Aye, we gon ride with' my bitch and we can come back later to pick up our rides."

I nodded my head in agreement and got out of my car. As soon as Marcus turned his back to me, I grabbed my other gun from the side panel and pushed it down to the waist of my jeans. Just in case things didn't turn out as planned.

****

TYCK

"Yo Tyck, what's good my man? Where yo' fine ass sister at?" Swag T asked me when he and Toe Tag pulled up beside me. I had been sitting out front of my sister's crib trying to catch some fiends to make a few dollars off of, and waiting for Feelow to get home. He had been gone for a couple of days and I was anxious to know where he had been. I kept imagining him running up on Marcus or one of his crew but I knew they were strapped and ready if he did.

I answered Swag with slight sarcasm in my voice. "Girl, her ass is up in the crib waiting on yo' ass to grow a dick." Toe Tag laughed but Swag didn't find shit funny. She cut the ignition off and got out but before she walked off, she said, "Yeah, but even without a dick, my nuts are still bigger than yours." I didn't pay her any attention when she walked past me and up the stairs to holla at Tykita. When my sister let her in and shut the door, I just shook my head and laughed.

"Aye Tyck, come here and let me holla at you for a second, "Toe Tag hollered from the vehicle.

I got up and walked over to the car and when I got there, he motioned for me to get in with him. I hadn't given him a reason to try anything crazy, so I got in the driver's seat where Swag had sat. After I closed the door behind me, Toe Tag asked, "Where the fuck is Marcus at?"

I shook my head and said "I ain't seen that nigga in a minute. You know he got that white bitch and now he is too good to hang out with us lower muthafuckas. Bitch done put him on a pedestal."

"Yeah. Damn, that white bitch got him like that? Shit, maybe I'll keep her around after I kill his ass then," Toe Tag stated with conviction.

Marcus had never done me dirty and he was the reason I had money in my pocket; he even kept it real after I told him about me and Feelow bumping dicks from time to time. He was just straight up loyal like that and even though Feelow had betrayed him, he still loved that nigga like a brother. My mind told me to let Toe Tag keep believing that Marcus had been the one to kill Carla but my heart told me to tell the truth and save the realist nigga I knew.

"Tag, I need to tell you something and you may not believe me at first but Marcus ain't do shit to Carla. It was ya boy Feelow," I stated in a hurry just so I wouldn't have second thoughts.

He looked at me with his brow scrunched and said, "Fuck that nigga. It's too late to try and protect him. You think I believe that shit about Feelow. Man Fee has been helping us keep tabs on that nigga. Ain't no way he would have done some shit like that and then put us up on his boy. You crazy as fuck if you think I believe that."

I couldn't believe that Toe Tag thought I was using Feelow as a cover-up to save Marcus, so I decided to give him my proof. I said to him, "Now you know Feelow and Marcus ain't been right for a while. Why do you think he's agreed to help you with murking Marcus? He's doing that shit so you'll trust him and save his own ass, but I got proof." I pulled out my cell phone and pulled up the video of Feelow torturing and killing Carla and passed it to

Toe Tag and stated. "You can watch the show for yourself, Here, check it out."

Toe Tag hit play on the video and the image of Carla began to play. The sound of her begging for her life brought tears to his eyes. He continued to watch and when he saw the blade slide across her throat, he cried out. "I'm gonna kill that bastard. He didn't have to do that shit to her. I knew that muthafucka was hiding something, I just never imagined it was this."

He passed my phone back to me and then pulled out his own and said to me, "Since you brought me this information after all this time, I should kill yo' ass right now but you lucky I'm feeling generous today. Don't tell Feelow that I know the truth. If you do, I'll come back for you. They don't call me Toe tag for nothing. However, I need you to keep acting normal around him until I can figure this shit out. Me and my crew are gonna do the same. I have to sit down with Echo and convince him to call a truce with Marcus."

I cut in and said "Man, Marcus ain't gonna let you kill Feelow. That nigga has been keeping him alive even after all this shit he's done. You gon' have to make that truce afterwards."

Toe Tag replied. "Yeah, you're right. But when I get through, it might just be Marcus who pulls the trigger on him." About that time, Swag T came down the stairs looking satisfied and said, "Nigga you in my seat. Get yo' ass outta my shit and tell your sister I said thanks for dinner."

I got out and started to walk away but Toe Tag stopped me and hollered, "Remember what I said, don't make me come back looking for you." The car pulled off and out of my line of sight. I shook my head and hoped that I had done the right thing.

****

CREEP

I walked out of the hidden room and out the back door so that I could go around the front to make it look like I had just gotten back from somewhere. As soon as I walked into the house,

Carrie's ass was on me. "Dammit Crestin, where the fuck have you been at and why the fuck you ain't call me? You got me out here looking like a dumb ass bitch checking for you and shit."

I put my hand over her mouth to hush her and said "yo ass needs to watch that mouth when you talking to me, you too damn pretty to be talking like a trucker and shit." When I moved my hand she said, "I'm sorry but I wouldn't be acting like this if you would have just kept your word to me. You can't just finesse me and then throw me to the side like trash."

I leaned down and kissed her pouty lips and asked "What's the matter girl? You missed daddy?"

She giggled and said in an innocent voice, "You know I've missed you. Daddy shouldn't have been so good to me got me tripping and shit. If you would just let me have daddy all to myself, I could be a good girl."

I then remembered something and asked "aye speaking of daddies. Ain't yo' daddy on the force?"

"Yeah, but what's that got to do with anything?" She asked innocently.

I responded, "I tell you what. When I get done putting this daddy on you, I'm a need you to talk to yo' real daddy and hook a nigga up. Shit, yo man be needing some protection out in them streets at times."

"Oh hell no, my daddy would shit on himself if he even knew that I was fucking with a dope boy. He would totally disown me Crestin," she said backing away from me.

"Oh yeah. Well, let's go back in that room and see if I can get big daddy to make you convince him otherwise," I said and brushed a finger over her lips. When she smiled and grabbed my hand, I looked over at Trap and mouthed, "We 'bout to be in there"

Marcus had been trying to find an officer on the force to work in the crew and feed us inside information and keep us from getting fucked up. We wanted to make the streets bleed cocaine on an even higher scale but we needed someone on the inside to wash our backs off whenever we got out on them. Had remembered

Carrie telling me when we first hooked up that her father was on the force but she had acted so damn crazy that I just didn't want to be fucked up with her. However, I had decided to take one for the team and try it again with her so she would convince her father to look out for us. I knew that it meant I would have to keep my dick at bay and only give it to her because if I fucked around with other bitches, it could mean prison gates or even death. I planned to be on my best behavior with her and hoped that I didn't get weak.

****

STANLEY EARL

Me and Thomas pulled up to Sarah's spot where we had planned to meet the nigga Ditto. It was a new place that she had purchased and it was in a decent neighborhood. I guess selling her pussy for dough had finally paid off. Sarah had been one of the few bitches who sold her goods to move up in the world instead of for drugs. She has spent her money wisely and she was smart. That's why I didn't mind fucking with her.

"Stan my man, you got yo' shit on you?" My right hand asked but I wasn't worried about being strapped because at the end of the day, Thomas had my back and he would stop any bullet sent in my direction, I replied, "Nah, don't feel like I need one. I ain't met a nigga yet that puts fear in my heart, plus I know you got me."

"Damn, right, I do my nigga and a muthafucka betta not test that shit," Thomas said as we proceeded up the stairway to Sarah's door. I wasn't the type of nigga who knocked on doors because I felt like my hands were too valuable. I needed them muthafuckas to count money and play in some pussy so I looked at my boy and nodded my head toward the door for him to knock. Thomas shook his head and said, "Bitch knew we were coming. A nigga feels like the door should a been open already."

"We should be able to see what we walked into, not stand out here guessing at that shit." I stepped to the side once I heard the locks being undone. Not because I didn't trust Sarah but because I didn't know the nigga inside waiting on me. Women tend to become blindsided after a good dick down and for Sarah's ass to be bold enough to call me about a stranger meant that he had slid up in her just right.

The only intentions she knew of were the ones he told her but he could have had a hidden agenda. My black ass wasn't scared of dying or doing a bid but I still had a little life to live, so I took caution until Thomas made sure I was straight.

"Damn Stanley Earl, I didn't think you were ever going to show up. Come on in so I can introduce y'all, shit," Sarah said after she had opened the door half naked. For a white bitch, her ass was plump and perfect and if I could get her in the back room before I left, I was gonna tap that shit. I had shown up late intentionally because I didn't know what I was going to step into. I had learned a long time ago that when you had a nigga waiting and didn't know what to expect, you had to throw they ass off. Being on time could be costly, so I always stayed unpredictable.

Me and Thomas followed Sarah into the living room where a slightly older cat sat on the couch. As soon as we entered, he stood up, making Thomas pull his piece. The nigga quickly held his hands up and said, "Whoa, whoa. Dawg, I come in peace. You ain't gotta do it like that" Sarah ran up beside him and said, "Stanley Earl, I give you my word, he's straight. Come on, you know I wouldn't have called you up on no bullshit."

Thomas looked from the nigga to me and I nodded to let him know that shit was cool and he could put his gun back. However, I knew that he would keep it handy just in case.

I sat in the chair opposite of the nigga that Sarah had called Ditto and listened to his story, "man, I had a little nigga under me and taught his ass everything but once his pocket got good a laced that muthafucka bailed on me. I've had a couple of his men hit but in turn, mine have been hit also but I ended up having to lie back for a minute so shit would die down. I hope them muthafucas think I'm dead but you know real niggas like me are hard to kill.

I'm trying to get back out there and eventually annihilate his young ass."

I laughed inside but kept a poker face while I absorbed what he had revealed. I didn't speak for a few minutes and it felt like time had stopped. I stated, " I guess I'm supposed to feel sorry for yo ass but I don't. However, I might be able it help you get back on your feet" I paused and looked at Sarah and then said "Yo Sarah, let me holla at you real quick. She looked from me to the nigga as if she had to get his permission but when I gave an order, bitches knew to comply. When she got up, I followed suit and together we walked to her back room. She already knew what was up and dropped her shirt. "Come on Stanley Earl, give me some of that good dick," she said seductively and then got on all fours, so I could beat the pussy up. I strapped my dick up and then slid inside of her and said, "If yo' boy ain't right, I'ma come back for you but I can assure you, it won't be for pussy."

Chapter Four
TOE TAG

"I'm gon' kill that lying muthafucka," I hollered and slammed my fist into the palm of my other hand. I was pissed at the news that Tyck had delivered and couldn't believe that I had been played. However, I had known that something about Feelow was off, but I never thought it would be something like that.

Swag T asked, "Man, what the fuck is wrong with yo' ass? What that nigga tell you? And it better not be no bullshit."

I replied, "It ain't just about what he told me. His ass showed me proof." I paused for a second, then continued. "He had us ready to point guns at Marcus for violation he didn't commit, and the bastard is gonna feel my wrath about my bitch."

"Wait, wait, wait. You are telling me that we were gonna shed blood in his camp and he ain't do shit against us. What the fuck?"Swag stated and then asked. "Did he tell you who really did it?"

"Bitch, you ain't caught on to shit I just said. I saw it with my own eyes and Feelow is gon' pay, Get Echo on the phone and tell him we are stopping the run on Marcus," I said with deep anger in my voice.

Swag T replied, "I ain't know Tag. Shit just might be too late. Echo already got that hit planned and you know when he makes plans, he doesn't change them for nobody.

I pulled out my phone and said, "Fuck that. I know I'm a muthafuckin' street nigga but I ain't never been coldhearted. I don't have innocent blood on my hands especially behind another man's sin. I don't need that Karma on my back." I dialed Echo's number and when he answered, I said, "Nigga, we are stopping the run on Marcus."

"The fuck you mean? I ain't calling off shit. That muthafucka has violated in more ways than one and his ass gonna pay. You have lost yo' damn mind or something?"Echo said angrily.

"Yo' man, Marcus ain't have shit to do with Carla's death. It was that nigga, Feelow. He snaked his ass up under us and convinced us it was Marcus but I saw the shit with my own eyes. You gotta stop that run," I said in an anxious voice.

The line was quiet for a couple of minutes and then Echo finally said, "Yeah bring me proof and then, I'll see what I can do."And then, he hung up.

****

KRYSTAL

I looked in the rearview mirror at the dude in the backseat that Marcus called Feelow. Something about him was very familiar but I just wasn't able to put my finger on it. I remembered him from the apartment Marcus had taken me to but it was more than that. The warmth of Marcus' hand on my thigh broke my chain of thought. "Aye, where ya mind at right now?" he asked in a sincere voice.

"Just thinking about the shitty life I used to have and how much better you have made it."

The smile on his face was priceless and I could tell that I'd boosted his ego up a notch but honestly, his ego didn't mean shit to me at least not anymore. I held a deep love for Marcus but I'd lost my respect for him long ago. "Oh yeah, well, I'm about to make it even better. You gon' be that bitch and I'm gonna make the whole world bow down to you when I'm done. Your pale white ass just better make sure you are ready."He said as he squeezed my thighs.

It was as if we were all alone in the car but Feelow suddenly made his presence known and said, "Yo, Dawg, look like snow done made yo' black ass soft" His light chuckle caused goose bumps to form on my skin but I ignored them.

Marcus said "Nah Fee. This snow bunny makes a nigga like me even harder and I mean always." He then let my thigh go and said," Turn right at this light up here and then go all the way to the bottom of the hill"

I did as Marcus told me to do and when I got to the bottom of the hill, I pulled into the driveway of the only house I saw the lights on. All the rest of them were boarded up and seemed to be abandoned at first but as I looked closer, I could see the flicking of small lights. I wasn't sure of what I'd seen so, I asked, "Marcus, why do I keep seeing lights flicker on and off in those abandoned houses?"However, instead of Marcus, it was his boy that answered me," Chill out white girl, that's just the fiends getting they smoke on. Come on and I'll give you a little tour while Marcus goes in and prepares the boys for your intro."

I looked at Marcus and he nodded his head at his boy and said, "That's a good idea. Go head on baby. You wanna be a boss bitch so you gonna see a lot of shit you ain't never seen before. Don't worry, you are in good hands. I gotta go in here and let my boys know what's going on before you take your position."He then walked away and left me with Feelow.

****

FEELOW

I couldn't understand why the white girl actually thought that she was ready to live the life of a boss. I for damn sure wasn't going to take orders from a cracker bitch. Marcus had me fucked up if he thought I was going to report to her. I hoped that by her seeing what went on in a street nigga's world, she would change her mind and pull out. When we got to the front door of the house a few feet from traps, I opened the door and held out my hand, and said, "Welcome to the real world."

She looked at me like I had two heads and stated, "You want me to just walk up in there without any kind of warning?" I laughed at her and then shook my head before I brushed past her and walked into the house. I then turned around to make sure she had followed.

The smell of the crack smoke made my stomach bubble and caused me to bite the inside of my jaws. I wanted a hit so bad I thought I would shit on myself. The fiends looked up at us but their activity never ceased. It was their choice to live the way they were but as long as it kept my pockets laced, I really didn't give a fuck. I heard the white girl say barely above a whisper, "Oh my God, this is so unreal."

I looked toward the direction she looked and saw a trick on her knees sucking a man's dick. The man that stood in front of her sucked on a dick himself-- a clear glass one that contained the very thing that she craved. I asked Krystal, "What's the matter, white girl? Ain't you ever seen a man get his dick sucked before? That's what they'll do for a hit of that shit. Hell, bitches will suck a dog's dick as long as that pipe stays full. You wanna try some of it?"

She looked at me in disgust. "This is really a sick way to have to live. Why don't you help these people instead?"

I couldn't help but laugh at her suggestion and then responded to her comment. "Help them? These muthafuckas don't want no help. They made the choice to live like this. If they don't get it from us, they'll hit a corner and get it from somebody else. How the fuck do you think you gon' be in this game and have compassion for a bitch who will let anybody with just a crumb of that shit fuck her for hours? You can't give a fuck about somebody who doesn't even give a fuck about themselves. Bitch, you better man the fuck up or move the fuck on."

Just as I'd gotten the words out of my mouth, a good friend named Johnny walked up and stated, "Fee man, let a nigga get a hit man. Shit, you know I'll take care of you. Come on." I started to curse his ass out but thought about it and said to him as I unzipped my pants and then pulled my dick out. "Yeah, aiight. A nigga could use a quick nut." As soon as the fiend put my dick in his mouth, the white girl turned around and walked out. I pulled back and when I did, Johnny asked, "What's up Fee?" I said to him as I dropped a fat rock in his hand, "Yo, you can make up for this shit later. I gotta go."

I ran out of the house and caught up to Krystal and said, "Look, I know you ain't ready for no shit like this so, the best thing for you to do is to pack up yo 'shit and go back where you came from. Your privileged white ass don't know shit 'bout the things we niggas had to do to come as far as we have. Bitch, we had to grow up and watch our mommas and aunties doing shit like them bitches in that house were doing. After a while, the shit just don't bother you anymore. I'm telling you that this kind of life ain't for you. So, take yo' ass on and let Marcus get back to the real world." I walked away and left her where she stood.

****

MARCUS

"So, let me get this shit straight, you are telling us that a white girl gonna be doing the pickups and drop-offs? You have lost yo' damn mind. What the fuck are you gon' be doing while she out here overseeing your product?"Creep asked with slight concern in his voice.

"I gotta lay low for a minute. At least until the shit with echo and Ditto, if he's still out there passes over. Nigga, I'm trying to stay alive right now. Besides, Fellow gon' be backin' her up until I get back in the front line."I stated.

"Feelow, now I know you've lost it. Why in the fuck would you put that nigga back on yo' right side when you know for a fact that all this street beef you got going on is because of him? Damn, man, you're crazier than I thought. But you know what? That's why I fuck with you."Trap commented with a small chuckle.

A knock sounded at the door and Trap nodded his head towards it to let creep know it was good to answer it. When he opened it, Feelow walked in and Krystal walked in slowly behind him. As soon as she saw me, she quickly walked over and acted as if she'd been spooked by something. I asked her, "Are you alright? Everything went okay out there?"

She stated with a half-smile, "Yeah, yeah. It was just different than anything I've ever seen but I'm good. I got this."

"Aiight, then, it's time you meet two of my men. This is Trap and Creep. Guys, this is Krystal, and she's the one who you will be dealing with for a little white. I'll still be on the scene but not as often until things die down," I said with a raised brow.

Creep shook his head and started to say something but another knock stopped his words. He went back to the door and opened it and that is when all hell broke loose. "Where the fuck is she, Crestin? Huh? I just saw the bitch walk through that door so don't fucking lie to me." Carrie's crazy ass hollered while she looked around the room. When her eyes finally stopped on Krystal, she said, "There she is. Bitch. Who the fuck are you?"

I started to say something but Krystal cut me off and held her own, "I'm the muthafucking Boss Bitch and I suggest you watch yo' mouth before I put something hot in it."The entire room was quiet and shocked as they witnessed Krystal turn from an angel to a beast in a matter of seconds. The bitch had just shown them that she was ready for street life but we all wondered if the streets were ready for her. I guess there was only one way for us to find out.

****

KRYSTAL

The days turned into weeks and the weeks into months and then out of nowhere, the years faded away behind me. Every day that passed without hearing from Marcus caused another piece of my heart to break away and I knew that eventually, I would have no heart left. I tried to wrap my mind around his reason but there were none to wrap it around. That bastard had left me for dead. Even after all I had done for him.

I felt that I no longer had a reason to exist in the world and so, I saved up packs of pain medication and when I thought I had enough, I took all of them but it didn't turn out as planned because I survived. I was pissed at God for letting me continue to live.

I didn't trust them and thought that all of them were out to get me. I was picked on and ridiculed but fuck them because them bitches didn't know the real story, but if I did make it out, they would one day hear about it, and they would envy me because I was a real bitch.

I thought back to the days I'd spent with Marcus. The good ones and the bad. He'd taught me things that a girl like me should not even know. I was groomed to run with the best of them and my shot was lethal.

I wondered if he even thought about me from time to time or had someone else occupied his mind. A bitch that sat beside him and thought she could replace me. The very thought of it made me clench my fists and caused chills to cover me. I still had time left and I'd decided that instead of feeling sorry for myself, I would use it wisely. It was time to man up and be the Boss that I was groomed to be.

Corey Robinson

Chapter Five
STANLEY EARL

"Aye, I need you to get out there and find out what's really up with that cat. Some shit just feels off to me," I said to Thomas after we'd gotten back from the ride.

"Yeah, Stan. I was sitting here thinking the same thing. That nigga had been hiding out and shit so, that means a muthafucka is looking for him really hard." Thomas stated and pulled out his phone. He talked for a minute before hanging up.

"Yo who was that?"I asked him once he'd completed his call.

Thomas stated, "That was a Lil nigga I used to run with when I was a kid actually beside you my friend, he's the realest nigga I know."He paused to gather his thoughts and said, "Aye, I'm stepping outta town for a couple of days but if you need me, holla and I'll step right back."

"Outta town. Nigga I'm trying to find out what's up with a muthafucka before I do bad business and you are talking 'bout you need to step outta town," I said to him angrily, and then asked, "Where the fuck you got to go on such short notice, T?"

"Damn Stan, chill out man. I'm going to find what you are looking for," he stated.

"How the fuck you gon' do that?"I asked.

Thomas said confidently, "I'm going to where the nigga came from."

****

KRYSTAL

"Crestin, are you really going to allow her talk to me that way?" Carrie asked while she looked at Creep to rescue her. When he didn't say anything to her, she added, "Mother fucker I can't believe your ass. Oh my God. I'm glad my daddy said no to backing your ass. I'm getting out of here."

No one spoke as Carrie turned to leave and right before she grabbed the doorknob, I said, "No, you should stay, I like your attitude and I think you could be very beneficial."

Marcus and all his men looked at me sideways but I didn't care because if I was going to be a boss, I wanted my own people too. Someone who would be hard enough to stand with me. Carrie seemed like a thorough bitch although I didn't know anything else about her.

"Krys, what the fuck are you doing? Have you lost yo' damn mind? The last thing you need is that crazy bitch on the team," Marcus stated, and then, his friend, creep said, "Shit, another crazy muthafucka on the team might actually be helpful dawg, think about this for a minute. Muthafuckas won't even see it coming until it's too late for their ass. They can be in the front line and we'll be in the back doing our thing." Trap said, "I agree. Our rivals would never expect it and so, we would always be one step ahead of them. I think your girl is right, Marcus."

I raised my eyebrows at him and then looked back to Carrie. She shrugged her shoulders and said, "I guess I could be helpful however you need me."

"You know how to use a gun?" he asked.

Carrie chuckled. "A gun? I don't need a gun when I got Hey-man and Karma. Together, they're more deadly than all your guns."

"The fuck is a Heyman and Karma?" Marcus asked.

Creep answered his questions. "Man, that's her mastiffs, and them muthafuckas are just as crazy as her ass but she's right, they are deadly as fuck."

"Aiight. I'll tell you what; you and your dogs are in but yo' ass gotta learn all the ropes including how to shoot," Marcus told her.

Carrie looked at me and said, "Okay, let the lesson begins. I'm ready when you are. I gotta be careful though because if my daddy finds out, he is going to cut me completely out of the will."

I didn't laugh at her comment because right then was not the time for it. Instead, I replied, "Just so you know, this only makes us business associates, we are not friends and if you stab me or anyone else on this team in the back, I'm going to kill your ass and I can assure you, daddy won't be able to save you, and neither will your mutts."

****

THOMAS

"Yo P, what's good man? Shit, it's nice to see you again," I said when I walked into the restaurant we'd agreed to meet at. Paris and I had been friends since we were little kids. We had bonded so easily because we'd had something in common. Both of our mothers had been murdered at the hands of men that they loved, leaving us to grow up without them. Our fathers had also been in prison at the same time. However, his dad had been released while mine was still doing time for murdering the man that took my mother away. Although, we lived in different cities now our bond was still solid.

"Thomas man, shit, it's good seeing you, dawg. I wish you'd consider coming back home for good." He embraced me in a brotherly hug. Although it had been many years since my mother's murder, the pain was still raw, and going back to the very place it happened brought back those awful memories.

I replied, "Nah man, I can't come back. Every time I think about walking down those streets I can see my momma's body. On those same streets I can see my momma's body laid out on the concrete. Shit ain't gonna never go away."

"You go see your pops lately?" Paris asked in a genuine voice.

"Yeah, I try to take my black ass up there every couple of months but it fucks me up every time I have to see him like that. He doesn't deserve to still be sitting behind those gates but I guess I gotta be thankful that he ain't on death row. However, I'll never stop trying to get him released," I said painfully.

"Yeah nigga, yo' pops has always been a muthafucking sol-dier, but it's time them crackas let him go. Shit, he did them a favor by killing Silas' evil ass. They should've given him a medal instead of a sentence," Paris said while he shook his head in disappointment at the thought of my father's incarceration. He then asked, "So, what brings you back this way man? Whatever you need, I got you."

I replied, "I need some information on a cat from around this way. Nigga trying to get some start-up from Stan but shit just don't feel right about it so, before I let my boy make a wrong turn, I'm trying to find out what's at the end of the street. Know what I mean?"

"Oh, Stanley Earl. Damn, I can't believe that nigga done blew up the way he did. I thought that muthafucka was gonna hit big on the R&B scene. But he hooked up with a hoe and took over the damn city. I'm proud of his real black ass, ask that nigga what's up? Shit, I feel like I should come over and join y'all," said Paris.

"Yeah, that nigga knows he can sing but he sells pussy and slang dope even better. Besides you, he is the only nigga that holds a place in my heart. I'll kill a muthafucka bout y'all. Man, if you came and joined the team wouldn't anybody ever be able to do shit with us. You know you are always welcome wherever I'm at."

"I know dawg. If it wasn't for my pops, I'd be gone. But anyway, maybe I could help you out with the information you need. What's the muthafucka's name?" Paris asked.

I looked him in the eyes and answered his question, "Ditto."

****

PARIS

As soon as he said the name, my heart skipped a beat. "You said *Ditto*?" I asked Thomas just to be sure I'd heard him correctly.

Thomas replied. "Yeah, man. Nigga said the streets call him Ditto. You heard of him?"

I took a minute before I responded because honestly, I was at a loss for words. I had been waiting impatiently for that nigga to pop up and now, he had fallen right into my lap. I finally gathered my words and said, "Yeah. I know that nigga. Actually, I used to work for him. That's the muthafucka that killed my momma. Pops hooked up with him when he was released from prison but it took him ten years to avenge my momma's death. However, that bastard seems to keep on fuckin' breathing"

Thomas replied, "Damn nigga, I'm sorry about that. We got a crew that can handle the shit for y'all. Hell, I'll break that mutha-fuckas back for you if you want. Shit, I knew something was off Thomas picked up his cell to make a call and said, "Yo, I'll call Stan right now and tell him to get the men ready. We gon' take this muthafucka out before he gets too comfortable." I put my hand over his phone and said, "Nah man, don't call nobody. This shit with Ditto and me is more personal. That bastard killed the only woman I could see spending my life with while she was pregnant with my seed. So, I may need you to let his ass get as comfortable as you can, and when he thinks shit is sweet, I'm making his life sour."

****

TUCK

Damn, sis, you fuckin bitches now?" I asked Kita when I walked through the door. She was in the kitchen cooking. She turned to me with her hand on her hip. "Fuck you Tyckori. It's my pussy and I'm gon' do what the fuck I wanna do with it. Besides, Swag treats me better than any nigga I have been with."

"Oh yeah? Then why are you still taking dick too? If she treats you that good then maybe you should stick to just pussy," I said while I stuck a spoon in the spaghetti sauce to taste it.

She slapped my hand away and said, "Yeah, so that way you can have all the dick to yourself. Nah, I'm greedy and want the best of both worlds, maybe you should try that too."

"Hmmm," I said with a smile, "nah, pussy ain't never did shit for me but push me out. I'm good, but thanks for the advice." I walked out of the kitchen and down the hall to the room. Inside, I picked up the phone and made a call. The line on the other end rang twice before it was answered.

"What up Tyck? You called just in time. You should come over to Traps so you can join in one of the festivities," Feelow said. I could hear different voices in the background but the main one that stood out was Marcus's.

I asked, "Yo nigga, you and ya boy good now?"

"We have somethin', but exactly what, I don't know right now. Why don't you come pick me up? We might be able to go somewhere else and chill for a minute. You sound like something's on your mind anyway," Fellow said as the other voices slowly faded.

"I think that's a good idea. I got to talk to you about something anyway and I can assure you that it's something you'll want to hear." I had a plan already made up and slowly it would come together. I just hoped I got the ending I truly wanted.

****

B-LINE

"Yo B, what's up with you man? Ever since shawty snow left, your ass has been quiet as fuck," Jambo said to me as I sat in a daze and thought about Krystal.

No matter how much I tried to convince her to leave Marcus, she still stood strong beside him. I looked up at my right hand and said, "Man, I'm good, just got a lot of shit going on in my mind."

"Oh yeah? Nigga, I think you're lying. I think it's your heart that's got shit going on. You wanna talk about it?" Jambo replied.

He and I met when we were in high school and found out that we were fucking the same bitch. When the word got out, everyone was ready for a fight that never happened. Real recognized real, and we decided to link up and keep fucking the same bitch. When she found out what we were doing, she left both of our asses alone and we never looked back.

With my dad so heavy in the dope game, I asked him if I could pull Jambo in as my lieutenant and we'd been thick as thieves ever since. Jambo seemed to feel the shit I was feeling so, I could never hide shit from him. I said, "Nah, talking ain't gonna change shit. She ain't gonna leave that nigga because she feels like she owes him her life. Ain't no way for me to make her see that he's going to ruin her life. If that muthafucka gave a shit about her, she wouldn't be riding dirty down the east coast. I just gotta sit back and let her find out for herself."

"What if she never finds out?" Jambo asked.

I looked up at him. "Well, I guess I can't miss what I ain't never had, playboy."

Jambo shook his head in disappointment. "Damn B, a nigga don't wanna see you like this, though. Come on, let's go out and find some pussy to fall in. It'll take your mind off of this shit."

I stood up from my chair. "Pussy does seem to make shit better but I'll pass. A nigga wannn dip in something sweet as fuck, and I don't think I'll ever find any sweeter than hers."

****

KRYSTAL

"Fuck you, Crestin. Did you forget that my daddy is a detective? Don't you think he would have already taught me how to shoot a gun? I don't need you to teach me shit," Carrie said and then aimed her gun at the circled target.

Creep replied, "Oh yeah, then why yo' crazy ass holding the gun wrong? A two-year-old could hold the gun better than that. But go ahead and do yo' thang baby girl."

I could tell that they deeply cared for one another but understood that Creep couldn't keep his dick in his pants when it came to other women. I knew that birds of a feather flock together so I was certain Marcus would continue with his whorish ways.

Carrie and I had been going to the gun range with the crew for the past few days so we could all improve our aim up to par. Every time Creep tried to show Carrie the proper way to kill a bitch she swore her daddy had already taught her, but that bitch missed every target. I finally said, "Hey, Carrie, maybe you should just stick with your dogs like you've been doing. I guess shooting a gun ain't for everybody." The whole crew laughed at my comment but I was dead serious.

As the days passed, I became so good at hitting the target that I could do it with my eyes closed. "Damn girl, yo' ass gon' be a lethal muthafucka," Creep stated, which caused Carrie to flip the script.

"What the fuck are you complimenting the next bitch for? Huh, Crestin? I might not have an aim as good as her yet but I promise if I shoot your ass, I'm gonna make you feel it."

Creep shook his head. "Damn, Carrie, can a nigga get a break from yo' crazy ass antics? Yo' ass gotta stop tripping on me and shit. And you wonder why I go to the next bitch for peace of mind."

She placed her hands on her hips and replied, "Go ahead and go to the next bitch. You've done that before so I'm used to the disrespect. However, I won't put up with it anymore, and busting the windows out of your car is nothing compared to how I'm going to light your ass up next time. Maybe you should go to one of them bitchs now while I work on my aim so when I shoot your bitch ass, I won't miss it."

"You know what ... that might just be a good idea. I'm outta here," Creep stated and walked out.

Carrie was about to go after him but I stopped her and said, "Carrie fuck him. Let his ass go shit, we are about to do bigger things and don't need any distractions. His ass will be back."

"Yeah, you're right. I can probably aim better without him here anyway. Fuck his ass," Carrie said and then went to stand back in front of her target with a sad but determined look on her face.

Carrie was crazy as fuck and tripped on others for petty ass shit but I needed her crazy ass to be on my team. We would never be friends because I refused to get close to a bitch but Carrie was a true rider. She would be perfect for those pickups that got out of line. I knew that some of the niggas we'd be delivering to would try our hand but with her crazy antics and my bold mind, no one would get anything past us. The only ones who could would be lying beside us at night.

****

STANLEY EARL

"Well, tell me, did you find anything out?" I asked Thomas as soon as Heather opened the door for him.

He walked in and sat down across from me. "Yeah, Stan, I found out more than I wanted to. My nigga, Paris apparently worked for that nigga and just like I thought that nigga foul as fuck, but I want us to deal with him anyway."

I couldn't understand why Thomas would want us to do business with a foul ass muthafucka. "Why the hell would you want us to take a chance with a muthafucka you already know ain't gon do right? That's crazy as fuck man."

Heather lit a blunt and passed it to me and then sashayed her fat ass out of the room. I hit it once and then passed it to my boy. However, before he hit it, he responded to my question, "Because I want him to trust us so my boy can get in."

"What the fuck yo' boy got to do with my shit? Answer that question for me," I said loudly.

Thomas pulled on the blunt and held his smoke for a minute before responding. "That nigga killed Paris' momma when he was a baby, then my nigga finally found love and that bastard killed her while she was pregnant with his seed. His ass don't know where Ditto's been until now. Paris, my nigga from way back; me and you gon' make sure he gets his revenge."

I could feel the depth of compassion he had for his friend in the pits of my soul. I also felt a little jealous at first but I knew that Thomas was real as they came and I knew that he held the same compassion for me and would ride with me through any beef that came my way. I might have been the boss but I always did what Thomas suggested because he'd never led me wrong. And this time would be no different.

I said to him sternly, "You've taken your friend's battle and made it yours, and any battle you got, I got." I paused and called out for Heather to come back in the room. When she returned, I said to her, "Call your cousin and tell her that everything went great on the sale of the boat. We'll drop off the keys to it tomorrow." She shook her head and then picked up her phone to dial out. I looked at Thomas, nodded my head, and said, "Vengeance will be ours. Call ya boy and tell him to keep his guns ready because we 'bout to send him a target." Then, I got up and went to load my own banger.

****

TOE TAG

"So, you are telling me that you saw the video of Carla being killed and it was Feelow on the video, not Marcus?" Echo paced the floor.

I said, "Yeah, I saw that shit for my damn self. Nigga, we had a target on the wrong muthafucka. I also found out through another source that his bitch ass sucks the glass dick. He had that secret buried deep as fuck but it's something we can use."

Echo said to Swag T, "Aye, I got an idea. Call ya people up in Brooklyn and get a batch of that shit with that ether cut in it. You say that nigga like to suck on that glass, so, let's fill that pipe up."

"Yeah, that shit sounds good and all but he ain't know that we know his secret so, he ain't gonna fall for that shit," I told Echo.

He looked at me and shook his head and then stated, "We don't need him to fall for anything. If that muthafucka is smoking that shit, then that means he gets high off his own supply."

Swag T cut in. "Yeah, so we just slip him a brick of that Brooklyn ether and the rest will be history."

"Exactly," Echo agreed.

I stated, "That sounds like a good plan but we need to make sure it's the brick of BK that he pinches off, otherwise, the shit won't work in our favor"

"And how in the fuck do we do that?" Echo asked.

"We go back and see that nigga Tyck. Them two niggas hang out together a lot. Muthafuckas probably bumping dicks or something but their bond can't be too tight if he's the one that told us to save Marcus," Swag said with a smile on her face.

We were all quiet for a second and then I said, "I'm bout to go back and pay that nigga a visit. Let's see how far he's willing to go to save Marcus. Swag, you make that call to yo' people while I'm gone and we'll meet back up here in a couple of hours."

"What? Nigga, you are crazy. I'm going with you. Shit, I could make that call from the ride. A little more time with Kita is just what I want. While you work on Tyck, I'll be working his fine ass twin," said Swag, getting up from his seat.

I shook my head and looked at Echo who in turn said, "Yeah, you go slide that bitch your plastic dick, and Tag, you get Tyck on board so he can get the right shit in that glass pipe."

I asked him, "And what are you gon' do while we handle this shit?"

Echo replied, "I'm gon' make sure these other bricks don't get wasted on his fuck ass. That muthafucka won't get the chance to make another dime off of my shit, and by the time he realizes something is wrong, it's gonna be too late.

****

TYCK

"Man, we have been held up in this muthafucka for a couple of days now and you still ain't told me shit. What the fuck is going on?" I asked Feelow as he blew smoke from his nose.

He sat quietly for a minute and then placed his pipe on the table and said. "That muthafucka got that white bitch holding my position while I sit on the backburner and watch. They were at the gun range shooting targets and shit. Bitch ain't even tried to contact me since he told the crew about her running things."

"So you mean to tell me that he is putting her over shit while he sits his black ass back and does nothing. So she gon' be making the deliveries and the pick-ups," I stated.

Fee replied, "Yeah, and that bitch has a VIP pass to the new connection which I'm having a hard ass time finding out who it is. I even tried to get that bitch followed one time but Marcus schooled that muthafucka very well. White bitch is smart as fuck"

I remembered the white girl very well, although Marcus didn't bring her around much. So, I wondered what made him all of a sudden change his mind and want to put her on front street. I had honestly hoped that once Feelow was eliminated, I could move up the ranks and take his spot, but now I had another roadblock in my way. I said to Feelow in a serious tone, "So, why don't you just eliminate the bitch?"

Fellow turned his head and looked at me. "Don't worry. I've already started up a plan to do just that but I'm gonna work alongside her for a minute first. Plus, she recruited Creep's ex-bitch Carrie to play along with her, and I gotta be real careful with that one. The last thing I need is for her fuck ass daddy to find out and come on the scene."

"What does her daddy have to do with anything?"

"He's a detective on the force and if he finds out Carrie is out here in that shit, he's gonna shut everything down, me included. I mean I like dick and all but a muthafucka ain't trying to go to prison to get it. Shit, I like my freedom too much.

I stayed quiet while Feelow put himself another hit on his stem. Once he had it melted, he laidback against the headboard and then struck the lighter. I listened to the drug as it sizzled and melted from the heat of the flame. As soon as he inhaled, his dick rose to attention. I stroked it for him while he held his smoke inside of his lungs for several minutes. He finally released it and said, "Come on Tyck, get this tension up off of a muthafucka. Make this shit in my head go away."

I stroked it one last time and then suddenly stopped. I let his dick go and looked up at him and said, "So you are saying that this bitch Carrie has a daddy that works on the force and would shut everything down if he found out she was out there like that?"

Fellow said in a frustrated voice, "Damn, man you act like yo' ass ain't understand it the first time. What the fuck is wrong wit' your ass? Man, I need you to get on this dick right now. That's all you need to worry about." When I didn't move, he asked, "What's on ya mind, Tyck. You look like a nigga with a plan."

I smiled and told him my idea. "Maybe his finding out that she's running with the crew would be a wonderful thing. You want that white bitch outta the way. Wait until she and Carrie are together and then give dear daddy a call. Quick and muthafucking easy and Marcus would never suspect you."

Feelow smiled at my suggestion. "That's a good idea. Now, come on and give me something else good. When I take my place, yo' ass is gon' sit on that throne beside me."

I was glad that Feelow listened to my plan but it was also one that I would let Marcus in on. If he knew that Feelow was trying to get his bitch hemmed up, he'd kill his ass for sure, and then, I'd finally be able to take my rightful place right beside Marcus.

Corey Robinson

Chapter Six
KEISHA

I had been waiting and hoping that Feelow would call me again although, I had promised Marcus that I wouldn't talk to him until he gave me the okay. A bitch was missing that nigga real bad and I was aching for him to share the experience of my pregnancy with me. I had already picked out a name for our little gangster, Khalif Keyshawn Feeland. It was a name that I was sure Feelow would love too.

I couldn't help but wonder how things went between Feelow and Marcus. I had only hoped that it went well so things could get back to normal. The birth of mine and Feelow's son was only a few months away and I wanted him to be present for the birth. I also wanted Marcus there because if it wasn't for him, I could have very well been out in the streets doing the same shit or for that matter dead.

I was bored and needed something to do so I decided against what Marcus told me and called a taxi. I had to get out of that apartment and find a piece of normalcy. Surely, shopping for baby clothes wouldn't bring me any drama. I would only be gone for a couple of hours and I would make sure to disguise myself so no one I knew would notice me.

When the taxi pulled up, I was already out front. I hopped in the back seat and gave him my destination. The closer we got to the mall, the more nervous I became but it was too late to turn back. When the driver pulled up to the mall, I paid him and got out. It felt really nice browsing the stores and there were so many people around that there was no way anyone could identify me. At least that's what I'd thought until I heard my name being called.

"Keisha. Girl, is that you?" I heard my cousin Tammy ask while I had my back to her.

I turned around and with a half-smile on my face. "Tammy, hey cuz. It's me."

"Bitch, why the fuck did you stop taking my calls? What the fuck is up with you?" I started to answer her but before I could get a word out, she beat me to it. "Bitch, are you pregnant?" she asked.

I had tried to cover it up the best I could but my belly had gotten so big that it was becoming hard to hide. However, if I would have stayed home as Marcus told me to, I wouldn't have had to hide shit. I knew that the encounter with Tammy could backfire.

I replied, "Um, yah. I done fucked around and got my ass knocked up. That's why I have been staying in and chilling."

"Girl, who the fuck are you pregnant by? Do I know the nigga?"

I said, "Well, you know I'm not sure who the father is. Girl, you know my ass was out there slinging pussy left and right. It doesn't matter anyway because we both know them niggas ain't shit." We shared a laugh and then I said, "Well, I got what I came for so I'm gonna get outta here. Take care, cuz. I'll call you soon."

"Yeah, you do that. Keep me informed about the baby. Hell, I wanna help spoil his or her little ass. You know you can always call on me," said Tammy.

"Yeah, I'll do that. I could use a helping hand once the baby's here. Thanks a lot. See you later." I leaned in to give Tammy a hug. There was no way I would tell her who my baby's daddy was. Tammy had always been jealous of me even though she claimed I was her favorite cousin. She was actually the only family I had that I still talked to but I knew she wasn't beyond stabbing me in the back. I could only hope that this time, with me being pregnant, she wouldn't push the blade all the way in.

****

TAMMY

I could tell that Keisha tried to disguise herself so that no one would recognize her. And it almost worked until she saw the butterfly ring on her finger our grandmother had given her on her sixteenth birthday. I had always hoped that grandma would give it to me and when she didn't, I had begun to hold a little animosity toward my cousin. Our mothers were sisters but Keisha's mom was always grandma's favorite so, she always got the most attention.

She had also always gotten the most attention from the guys. With her big ass, long hair, and hazel eyes, men flocked to her. I realized that was why Feelow had asked about her, and I wondered if he knew she was pregnant. I had been begging Feelow for the dick and he would never swing it my way.

When I finally got him to give it up, he had asked me about Keisha. I was pissed at the thought of that muthafucka using me to get to her so I decided to give him a call.

When I dialed his number, he picked up on the first ring, "Yeah, what's up? Who's calling?" he asked, and then I went the fuck off.

"Muthafucka, is that *your* baby my cousin Keisha is carrying? You fucking bastard! You used me so you could get her number, didn't you?"

"Ah come on now, Tammy. You know a nigga ain't doing it like that, so stop tripping," he replied.

"Then why did your ass wanna get her number and call her so bad?"

"Girl, that bitch owed me some fucking money and I'm not talking about a few dollars. I need my bread from that hoe, that's all. Anyway, why are you questioning me about her? Did you see that bitch somewhere?"

"I might have. If I tell you where I saw her what's in it for me?"I asked seductively and hoped he would catch it.

"Shit girl, you know this dick hard just from hearing your voice. Just tell me where she at and this muthafucka gon reward that ass later on," he promised.

My pussy throbbed at the thought of Feelow fucking me again and having a wet pussy and a weakness for good dick had my ass talking. "She was out here at the mall shopping for baby clothes and was trying to disguise herself but I know that bitch anywhere. As a matter of fact, I see her now. She's still out front, probably waiting on a ride." I said while I looked out the entrance of the mall.

Fellow stated anxiously, "Tammy, go out and stall that bitch for as long as you can. I'm on the way." He hung up abruptly.

I looked at my phone crazy-like and then finally pushed the end button. I put my phone in my purse and walked out to stall Keisha. I only hoped that it would work because a bitch couldn't wait to have Fellow back inside me. I was going to do everything in my power to keep Keisha from leaving.

****

FEELOW

I had laid up with Tyck for the past few days while Marcus and his bottom trappers took the girls to the shooting range. I figured I could get some dick and a good high and try to process the shit Marcus had pulled. But as luck would have it, the call from Tammy made shit a little easier to take. When I hung up the phone, I turned to Tyck and said, "I gotta go. My bitch is at the mall and I need to get there before she disappears again."

He stated, "Well damn, Feelow, you just gonna leave me hanging like that for a bitch who doesn't want to be bothered with yo' black ass. You need to decide if you want a bitch or a nigga because this shit is getting old."

I looked at Tyck like he had grown two heads. "You sounding like a bitch and a nigga all in one, so if this shit is too much for you, push the fuck on. Muthafucka, I can't let the streets know that I like dick. Every block out there would lose all respect for me if they found out so do what you need to do. Either ride or drive down another road. The fuck you thinking?"

Tyck remained silent while I got dressed but right before I walked out the door, he said, "Nah man, you right. I'm just tripping. Dick shouldn't be so damn good and then I wouldn't mind sharing it. I ain't gon' trip no more Fee. Just go handle yo' business and holler at me when you are through."

"Yeah, aiight." I walked out and slammed the door behind me.

I got in my car and sped off. I hoped Tammy was able to stop Keisha from leaving the mall. The only way I would hold back was if it was Marcus that would be picking her up. I wasn't willing to wait and find out so I decided to call Marcus and find out if it was him or if he was still with the white bitch.

"Aye what's up, dawg? Where the fuck you at, man? I need yo' ass out here with me, helping me get these bitches ready," he said as soon as he answered. I was glad to know that he was still out training his underlings.

I said, "Yeah, I had a couple of things to take care of, and then I ran into this bitch I use to fuck with. Man, when I dipped in that fat pussy, I just couldn't bring myself to pull out. I stayed up in that shit till my dick was drained."

Marcus laughed. "Shit man, I know exactly how good pussy will do a nigga. That *wap* will have a muthafucka paralyzed. It's all good though. We only gon' be out here a couple of more hours and then, we gonna take it on in. I'm gon' send Krystal out tomorrow and start her up. I'm anxious to see how everything goes."

"Ah man, I think that little snow bunny gon' do aiight. Plus, she sent that crazy ass Carrie out to patrol the top. I think you gon' be happy with the outcome," I said, although I hoped the bitch fucked all his money up.

"Fee man, you don't feel no type of way about me putting my girl out there to handle some shit, do you?"

"Marcus, come on man. This type of shit ain't gon' put a dent in what we just repaired. I'm just glad that I got my brother back. I'm wit' you no matter what." I stopped talking because I had pulled up in the mall parking lot and saw Keisha walking beside Tammy on the way to Tammy's car. "Aye yo, Marcus," I said quickly. "I got to go in this store for a second, so I'm out. I'll catch up with you in a minute. Peace."

I waited until Tammy and Keisha got in the car and then pulled behind it to block them in. When I got out, I heard Keisha say loudly "Holy shit! Bitch, you set me up!" Keisha then opened the door and grabbed her things. When she stepped out of the car, we were face to face. This bitch would not get away from me again. "Feelow, what are you doing here?" Keisha asked nervously.

I looked down at her bulging belly. "I wanted to see you and talk to my son. Come on, Keisha, give a nigga a chance. You know yo' pretty ass miss me."

About that time, Tammy came around the car and put her hands on her, spewing, "I thought you said she owes you money and you wanted me to help you collect. Now you are telling her to give your ass a chance. I knew I shouldn't have trusted you."

Keisha turned to Tammy and said, "Bitch, you called and told him I was here? Is that why you stalled me in the Uber and then offered me a ride? You're supposed to be my family but you're a fucking snake!"

Tammy looked from me to Keisha and then spat, "Bitch, fuck you and that dirty dick nigga. His ass wasn't thinking about you and that bastard you carrying when he was draining the juice outta this pussy. You always thought you were better than me. I ain't never gave a fuck about you. You two muthafuckas deserve each other. I ain't fuckin' with neither one of y'all. I'm outta here." She turned and got in her car but I had her blocked in, so she hollered out, "Nigga, you got two seconds to get that piece of shit out my way!"

I took Keisha by the elbow, saying, "Come on and get in the car. We have a lot of catching up to do." Keisha hesitated at first, but then she gave in and got in the passenger seat. I got in and before I pulled off I hollered out the window to Tammy, "You a dumb bitch if you thought I'd choose you over her. Bitch, you got played! Fuck you!" I pulled off with one destination in mind.

****

TYCK

I was pissed at that muthafucka for leaving me for a bitch who had been hiding from his ass. He had been looking for her for a minute and then found out that Marcus had her in a safe place. I remembered Keisha before I got locked up. She used to be shy until she got her first piece of dick and then, she turned into the neighborhood hoe.

Fellow had run into her one night and they hooked up, and that's how she ending up getting her pregnant. At first, he denied being the father, but I guess a man can feel some sense of empathy after a while to where he can no longer deny his seed.

I knew that Marcus was going to be pissed when he found out that Keisha was with Feelow. I wanted to call and tell him but I didn't want Feelow to know I had contacted him, so I would have to figure out another way for him to come upon the revelation. I had remembered Feelow telling me that Keisha's cousin, Tammy had a thing for him so he used her to get to Keisha. I decided that I'd use her too. I just hoped it would be easy, but I had to get her number first. I called the messiest bitch I knew, and she answered on the first ring.

"What the fuck are you calling me for, Tyckori? Couldn't the shit wait till you got home?" my sister Kita asked.

I replied, "It ain't like yo' ass is that damn busy. I just called to get a number from you sis. I'm trying to take your advice and try some pussy but I don't got the number of the girl. I know yo' ass knows everything so, can you help your brother out?"

I could hear Kita as she smacked the gum she had in her mouth and then, she asked, "Well, who is the bitch you are trying to holler at?"

I said, "Man I'm trying to get with Keisha's cousin, Tammy. They say that bitch head game is off the charts."

"Tammy," she snapped, "Why you wanna hit that tired ass hoe. You better off just sticking to niggas because that bitch is ratchet."

"Yeah, I know she ratchet but that's what I like about her. Shit why do you care you ain't gonna be fucking her, I am." I said and then waited a couple of minutes before Kita spoke again.

"Alright but if your dick falls off don't say I didn't warn your dumb ass," Kita stated and then gave me the number and hung up.

"Damn, my sister ain't shit."I said out loud and then dialed the number Kita had given me. The phone on the other end rang about five times and I started to hang up but right before I pushed the end call button, I heard a voice.

"Hello," the female said.

"Hey, I'm trying to reach Tammy. Is this who I'm talking to?"I asked.

She replied, "Yeah, this is Tammy. Who the fuck are you?"

I didn't want her to know who I really was so that way, she could never snitch me out so I said, "It doesn't matter who this is. Let's just say that I'm someone who is on your side."

"What the fuck are you talking about? Why don't you stop speaking in some dumb ass code and tell me why you are calling?"She stated with much attitude.

I said, "Aiight, I know you're pissed right now because Feelow dissed you for Keisha and I'm just trying to give you some ammunition to get some payback. Do you want it or not?"

The line went silent for a minute and then Tammy asked, "What's the ammo? That muthafucka used me and I'm down for whatever to make him and that bitch feel me."

I told her just what she needed, "Write this number down."

****

MARCUS

Hold the fuck up, Tammy, you are telling me that Keisha is with Feelow right now as we speak?"I asked when Tammy gave me the information.

"Yeah, I ran into her at the mall and remembered that Feelow told me she owed him a bunch of money and if I ran into her that I should call him. Well, his black ass lied, he was just trying to get to her because she 'pose to be having his bastard child. I can't even believe I fell for that shit. Anyway, that dumb bitch is with his sorry no good ass right now. I don't know where they went but I know they were together," Tammy said with deep satisfaction.

"Aiight Tammy, I'm gonna go see if I can locate them. Thanks for the knowledge. If you run into them before I do, call me immediately," I hung up and processed what I had just been told. It's not that I didn't want them together, I was just worried that Feelow would do something to Keisha and the baby she carried.

I couldn't believe that Keisha went against what I told her after all I'd done for her. Although me and Feelow somewhat made amends, there was a piece of me that still didn't believe that he was moving right. Plus, I knew in my heart that he felt some type of way about me putting Krystal in his spot even if it wasn't permanent.

I wasn't sure what state of mind Feelow had been in the past couple of days so, I couldn't determine the outcome of him and Keisha's encounter. I picked my phone back up and decided to call Keisha just to see if she would tell me the truth about where she was. When her phone went to voicemail, I called Feelow and he answered on the second ring.

"Yeah nigga, she's with me so you can stop looking for her. What? You thought I wasn't gonna find out that you had my bitch and my namesake hidden away from me?" Feelow said as soon as he answered.

"Fee man, a nigga was only trying to protect her and your son. Yo' ass was on a murder mission and I didn't want you to do something you'd regret. I just wanted to make sure she was safe until you came to your senses,' I said in a genuine voice.

Fellow replied, "My senses, huh? All that shit you talked about us getting back like we used to be was just that. Shit! Keisha is back where she belongs now and if you come near her, it will all end for you."

My heart broke again with each word he spoke. I stated, "Nigga come on with that shit. What the fuck happened with us? What happened to us being our brother's keeper man?"

"Nigga, I'm an only child, there is no us," Feelow said right before he hung up.

Chapter Seven
DITTO

"Damn, what the fuck is taking ya boy's ass so long to get back with you? Nigga acting like he ready to lose out; like his ass don't wanna make no real money," I stated to Sarah, who was sitting on the couch while she painted her toe nails. She looked up at me and replied, "Real money. Nigga that shit you gon be paying Stanley Earl ain't nothing but pocket change and I can assure you that if he doesn't get it, he damn sure won't miss it so chill, he'll call."

"Bitch, I know you ain't taking up for that muthafucka. I'm the one pushing dick in you at night so yo' ass 'pose to be on my side of this. What the fucks up with that?'I asked and meant every word. True enough, I was only sticking around and making that bitch holler at night so I could get what I wanted. Once I got the connection to trust me, Sarah's pale ass would be history. I also didn't need a bitch who took another niggas side and could possibly turn on me.

Sarah said, "I'm taking up for him because I know him and since you trust that dick inside of me raw, your ass should be trusting my words. He'll call, just be patient."She then put her nail polish down and got up from the couch, and walked over to me. As soon as she put her hand over my dick, her phone rang. I looked down at her and said, "Go head and answer that. It might be that nigga. Then come on back over here and take care of this."I grabbed my dick through my sweatpants and caused her to smile and then, she went to answer her phone. Sarah was a good girl but I didn't have time or patience for a steady woman in my life, plus I had too much shit going on. Any bitch that rode with me was subject to losing their life because before I ate a bullet, I'd pull the bitch in front of me and make her swallow the lead instead.

I listened closely while she spoke into the phone," Okay. Alright, so, it's good then?"She listened intently to the person on the other end and then said, "Alright, we'll be looking for you. Oh and thanks." Then she hung up.

She turned to me and said, "Stanley Earl and Thomas are on the way over with ten keys to start you off. They should be here in about twenty minutes."

I smiled at the thought of having a new connect and I couldn't wait to get my hands back on the product. I had hoped for twenty keys but I knew that I would need to prove myself to the nigga before I could get more. I was about to get back on my feet in the game and couldn't wait to show my face again. Muthafuckas counted me dead, but little did they know I was still breathing. I decided that as soon as I got it in my hands, I'd reach out to Blackout and put him on. He was the only nigga that hadn't turned his back on me and I knew that a loyal muthafucka was hard to find.

I looked at Sarah and stated, "Twenty minutes."

She nodded her head and said, "Yeah, about that."

I pulled her to me and said, "Well, that gives you about nineteen to finish what you started."

She pulled down my sweat pants and then got on her knees and said," Nineteen. I'm about to blow the top off of this mother fucker," And then, she pulled me into her mouth.

****

STANLEY EARL

So, I'm gonna give him these ten keys on consignment and see how he does. When it's time to pick up my money and bring some more product, we'll send your boy in to get it. We'll make it like we had to go out of town and send in another worker. He'll never see that shit coming," I said to Thomas.

Thomas replied, "Yeah, but I think we should go ahead and tell him that he'll be dealing with someone else and see how he reacts to it. A nigga's expression says a lot about what he's thinking. Muthafucka might wanna make some plans if he knows that someone else is gonna come through instead of the boss man."

"See, T, that's why I fuck with you. That's some real shit you just said and it's a brilliant plan. He has no idea that you have an affiliation with a lil nigga that used to be under him. We ain't gonna let him know that we are sending in a seasoned nigga. Let's make him think he's going to be expecting a lower soldier in the ranks," I said while l pulled into Sarah's complex.

"I can't wait for that foul muthafucka to see Paris' face when he walks in to do the deal. That bitch is gonna shit in his boxers," Thomas said with a laugh and then asked, "Yo Stan, we gon put Sarah up on that shit so she doesn't get caught in the cross."

"Hell no, nigga! You know good dick makes a bitch weak. Her dumb ass shouldn't be fucking with a nigga she doesn't know. Bitch should have done some investigation first. That's her ass," I stated and then, shut my engine off.

"Boy, your bitch is gon' be pissed if something happens to her cousin," Thomas said as a matter of fact.

"Yeah, and like I said, a good dick makes a bitch weak. Her ass ain't leaving this anaconda. She might be mad for a minute but her ass will get back right real quick fuckin wit' me."

Thomas laughed and opened his car door to get out. I followed suit and when I slammed my door, I heard a voice from behind me. "Damn, I ain't think y'all niggas were gonna ever make it rain," Ditto said.

I looked at Thomas and noticed him put a hand behind his back but I didn't think the dumb nigga had any intentions of doing anything, at least not out in the open. Thomas asked him, "You sho' anxious to get your hands on this product."

"Nah, man, it ain't even like that. I had just stepped out for a minute and noticed y'all pull in. Shit, I'm just ready to get my life back," Ditto exclaimed.

I said, "Yeah, well, I'm about to give you a head start with that." I nodded to Thomas for him to pull the duffel bag from the hidden compartment. I made sure to walk away from the car first and walk with Ditto back to the stairs. I didn't need his snake ass knowing where my shit was stashed when I rode the streets. When niggas like Ditto got hemmed up, they wouldn't mind dropping a dime on someone else to help their own case. I had dealt with muthafuckas like him before but I was too smart to fail and I wasn't about to let his ass change that.

By the time we had got to the top of the stairs, Thomas was behind us with the product. Ditto opened the door and moved out of the way and gestured for us to walk in first but I wasn't about to turn my back on him so I said, "Nah, you go ahead. We are right behind you, player."

Ditto shrugged and walked in followed by Thomas and then myself. Anytime we walked into a situation my boy always went first. That was his rule because the nigga was thorough. He always said he'd take whatever the enemy had for me because he didn't think the world could keep turning without me in it.

"Hell, y'all, a bitch gotta go out for a minute and get some food to put in here but I'll be back in a little while," Sarah said and grabbed her purse and keys.

Me and Thomas looked at each other and then I said, "Yo, Sarah let me holla at you real quick before you step out. It will only take a minute."

"Alright come on and walk me outside." She looked at Ditto and their exchange made me a little uneasy but I brushed it off because I trusted that Sarah wouldn't plot against me, and prayed that I was right.

"Look, I hope you ain't been telling that nigga shit because you don't know that muthafucka, and I'm a man so, I know how to tame a bitch when I want to," I said as soon as we made it outside.

"Stanley Earl, I might be a hoe but I'm not a dumb bitch. His dick is good but nigga it ain't that damn good to make me be disloyal. His ass been digging and asking questions but I have been playing stupid. I'd die before I'd do shit against you," Sarah said and then stood on her tiptoes and gave me a peck on the cheek. I knew that she was keeping it real but I still knew to be cautious. Sarah got in her car and when she drove away, I took my ass back upstairs so I could look the snake in his eyes.

****

DITTO

When that nigga, Stanley Earl walked back into Sarah's apartment, I looked him dead in the eyes. I could feel in my gut that he and his side kick didn't trust me and honestly, I didn't give a fuck. I just needed them to give me what would put me back on. I planned on getting those ten keys and pushing them out with the help of blackout. When they were gone, I was going to get ten extra and then tell these muthafuckas to kiss my ass. They could either accept it or get yanked. I would leave the choice up to them.

I asked, "So, y'all niggas are ready to do this business?"

Thomas replied, "Yeah, we are always ready to make those ends meet up. He then unzipped the duffel bag and pulled a kilo out and said, "You wanna check this for yourself?" He slid the kilo across the table to me."

I replied, "Well, you two seem like legit businessmen so, I'm hoping I don't have shit to worry about. I'm just ready to get started." Thomas slid the kilo back to himself but Stanley Earl put his hand over his boys and stopped him from putting it back in the bag and said, "Nah, legit or not you gon' test this kilo and the other nine in my presence so I can be assured that no fuck shit comes back to me."

The kilo was slid back over to me and then Thomas pulled out a small knife for me to use to test it. I cut a small slit into the package and then collected some of the cocaine on the tip of the blade and when the product touched my tongue, it became numb instantly. "Damn, this some potent ass raw. The fiends gonna be busting my door down to get some of this," I said while Stan took another kilo out of the bag.

It was the same routine with the other nine kilos and I wasn't sure if I'd ever be able to taste anything else on my tongue. I had never had cocaine that pure and was very pleased that there was no cut on it. "This shit straight as fuck. I dealt in some good cocaine but I think this has outdone all before it. What do I owe you?" I asked after I tested the last one.

Stanley Earl said, "You good. I'm giving you these first ten on consignment for eighteen a piece, anything over that, of course, is yours to do as you please. You know as well as I do that keys have been going for twenty-four so, you're going to make a sixty profit. How do you feel about that?"

"Sixty sounds great and it will get me back on my feet. I'll be able to give Snow back the space too and then eventually Show my face without worrying about my enemies, but man, I got some loot stashed. I mean I don't have a full one-eighty to give you up front but I got a little something," I said with a straight face although it was a lie.

"Nah, you good, we got to build up that trust, pman. You know what I'm saying? You do right on these ten and the shipments will keep getting bigger with the prices lower. However, this will be the only time I'll be in your presence. Next time and from here on out, you'll be dealing with one of my up-and-coming soldiers instead of me," Stanley stated.

Thoughts of malice went through my head immediately and plans were already being made. I said, "Alright, that's straight. I'll call when I'm ready for the re-up." Stanley Earl and Thomas got up from the couch to leave so I walked them to the door. I couldn't wait to put some cut on the cocaine I had been given. I was going to double that sixty thousand dollar profit even if it caused a few hearts to burst open, "Fuck, them muthafuckas," I said out loud after I shut the door behind them and locked it. Stanley Earl might have been the big dog for now but when I got finished, he would be walking around with his tail between his legs, and on a leash, one that I would be pulling on.

****

PARIS

I just couldn't believe how luck dropped that nigga right in my lap. I would lay awake at night and fantasize about all the ways I was going to kill his ass. That bastard was going to swallow a bomb this time. The shit made my dick hard just thinking about it. I started to turn over and try to get some rest but my phone stopped the slumber I so desperately needed.

"Who the fuck is calling me this time of night and whatever you want better be good," I said into the phone with a slight attitude but the voice on the line took it all away.

"Yo Paris, this is Thomas man. Shit has been put in place for you to make a move so you need to get it together and come on up and join me." I sat up from the bed really fast and could feel my heart pumping a couple of notches higher. This was the phone call I had waited for.

I said, "Thomas, are you for real? Man don't be playing with me about that shit."

Thomas replied, "Nigga when you have known me to play about shit like that. You are my man and I told you I got you, so get up and get yo' ass up here, muthafucka."

I didn't even respond, instead, I ended our call. Nothing else needed to be said. I knew what needed to be done now so I didn't waste any time. I got up and started to pack a bag and suddenly heard something behind me and when I turned around, I was face to face with my father.

"You are going somewhere son?"He asked as he looked around me at the bag I was packing. My father had never put fear in my heart but at the moment, I felt scared. The look he held in his eyes brought chills down my spine."Got a tip about that nigga and I'm going to see about it," I replied.,,,

"I know you son, and I know you ain't gonna move just on a tip. Where did you get your information from?"He asked with a serious and concerned tone. I knew not to lie to him so, I told him the truth.

"My boy Thomas and his boss happened to run across a nigga who needed a new connection. Before they deal with him, they wanted to find out about him and since this is where he came from, Thomas came down and asked me about him. When I asked him the muthafucka's name and he said the streets called him Ditto, pops, I could feel Torrie's arms wrap around me. It was like she had come back to me for a minute. I'm 'bout to head up that way so I can bring his ass down to size," I stated.

"So, you weren't gonna say shit to me about it?" he asked.

"Nah pops, I want to handle the shit on my own. I owe this to Torrie and my seed, I'm straight. I'll have Thomas with me just in case I need back up."

"You mean, the same Thomas you used to run with when you were young?"He asked.

"Yeah, the same one. I ain't seen his ass in years and I was happy as fuck when he told me. He ain't even know that I had a beef with that nigga until I told him so you can't tell me that this shit wasn't meant to be," I said with a smile on my face.

My father replied, "Well then, I guess we better pack up and get on the road then"

I caught what he said and asked, "What do you mean we? I got this, pops."

He turned and looked me in the eyes and stated, "When a beef comes this way, they ain't no me and no you. There's only an us and a we. Lil nigga, you are all I got left on this earth to live for and as long as I breathe air into my lungs, you will never fight without me. So, like I said, pack a bag and let's go kill that muthafucka."

****

DITTO

I was about to hang up when I heard someone on the other end of the line. "Hello?" a female voice said.

"Aye, bitch, put Blackout on the phone," I said.

"Nigga, who the fuck you calling a bitch? Muthafuckin coward-ass bastard. Fuck you," she hollered at me, and then I heard her saying something to Blackout. "Here, it's some bitch ass fuck boy calling for you. You better teach him how to fucking address me, nigga."

"Girl, shut the hell up and put this dick in yo mouth," Blackout said and then put the phone to his ear to hear what I had to say. He already knew that it was me because he had a ringtone that was used only for my calls. He asked, "Yo man, what's up on yo' end? Are you ready for me?"

"Yeah, I got ten feet of fishing line and I'm ready to reel in the fish. You ready to get on the boat?" I asked.

Blackout and I always spoke in code even when we were around the others that I had in my crew. That nigga was like a younger version of myself and I couldn't do anything but respect him. He had grown up around drug dealers all his life and when they were snatched from him, he was forced to live in the streets where he would take refuge to keep him out of foster homes.

"You know it my man. hit, a nigga already got his tackle box filled and ready. It's time to bait some of these hooks. Just tell me when and where and I'll be early," Blackout exclaimed.

I replied, "B you gon' have to make a trip outta town on this first one. Plus I need you to give me a full report before I step out. You got me?"

"Nigga, you ain't even gotta ask. I always got you," he said and then stated to the girl that was with him, "Damn, baby, you bout to make this shit start shooting. Fuck!"

"Hey man, go on and get ya dick off and I'll call you back tomorrow to let you know where the rivers are. Oh, and tell yo' bitch, I'm sorry," I stated and hung up.

"Mmm who were you talking to this late at night?" Sarah asked from beside me while she pushed her ass closer to my dick.

"Keep playing and wake that muthafucka up and yo' ass is gon be sorry," I said and slapped her on the ass, only causing her to giggle and turn over.

"You know I like begging, so why don't you punish me," she cooed.

She put her hand on my dick and began to massage its width. I looked down into her eyes and asked, "So, if shit gets foul between me and yo' boy, whose side are you going to take?"

She stopped massaging my dick and asked, "What kind of question is that Ditto? You know my boy is straight so how could anything go foul? Besides, you know I can't betray this good dick right here." She laughed but I wasn't in the mood for jokes.

I put a hand around her wrist and squeezed. "Yeah, that's yo' wet ass pussy talking right now but I'm being for real. I need to know whose side you're on in the end."

The room had got quiet and I could tell that Sarah was thinking hard about her answer. So, I stopped her from thinking for good. When my hand went from her wrist to her neck, her eyes grew wide. She knew what was about to happen but there was no way she could stop it. I looked deep into her eyes while she struggled to get my hand from around her neck but I wasn't going to let this bitch live another day not knowing where her loyalty stood. A bitch that's unsure would turn and I wasn't giving her that chance.

I squeezed harder as she fought and grew weaker. Eventually, her arms fell and her eyes froze open. I squeezed one final time to make sure I got her good. When her last breath left her body, I stared at her and thought about what I'd done. I knew that if her boy found out about it, there'd be hell to pay.

I decided that when I met up with him again, I would say that Sarah had stopped out for a minute but then, a better thought came to my mind. I picked up my phone backup and dialed Blackout's number again. When he picked up, I said, "Aye, you need to leave tomorrow and bring yo' bitch with you. I made a mess, too, so bring the cleaning crew. I'll tell you where to go from there." I hung up.

Chapter Eight
Crystal

"Aye baby, I'm gonna need you to make one more trip up to Baltimore before I find a replacement for those pick-ups," Marcus said to me as soon as I opened my eyes.

"Well damn, good morning to you too."I sat up in the bed and then said, "I thought those trips were over for me. At least that's what you're no good ass said."

Marcus walked over to the bed and stood in front of me with nothing but a towel wrapped around his waist but little did he know, his dick was no longer my weakness. That muthafucka had shared it with too many other bitches so to me, that shit was washed up. I stated with an attitude. "Uh, you can get that out of my face. I don't fiend for it like I used to. As a matter of fact, I can do without it." I stood up and pushed past him.

He followed behind me, asking "You fucking other niggas now?"

"Fuck you, Marcus. One thing I've never been was a whore, unlike *you* of course. I'm just as turned on as I used to be, but I still believe you park that thing in other garages, so I'm good. When I'm ready for some, I'll let you know." I went into the bathroom to take a shower and get ready for my day. It would be my first day actually out picking up the money from the trap houses. I would be on one side of town while Carrie would be on the other. We would each have a soldier with us just to make sure no one tried us although they all had been warned.

I had been thinking of recruiting Carrie to make the Baltimore runs instead of me but I was worried that she'd get too close to Brandon and the thought of him with someone else made my stomach turn. However, I would take her on this run with me and introduce her to Jambo instead. When I came out of the bathroom, Marcus was packing a duffel bag full of money. He looked over at me and said, "You should take Creep's bitch and teach her the ropes. Shit, all she got to tell a muthafucka is that daddy's a fuckin cop and she'll be home-free."

I nodded my head and replied, "Yeah, that's what I was just thinking too. I think she should be the one to replace me. Bitch has the attitude and the guts to make it without looking scared. I'll talk to her about it on the way up." I paused for a minute and then added, "But I don't think it's wise for people to know that her dad is a detective. Something like that could easily backfire and possibly get her killed or even in a hostage situation. You know people will go to the extreme to get them self out of trouble when they get hemmed up."

Marcus walked up closer to me and said, "You a smart bitch, you know what? I know you gon' handle this street shit like a real boss. Plus, you got a good teacher"

I kissed Marcus on the cheek and walked away from him and stated, "Don't give yourself too much credit because I may have taught you a thing too. You know what I'm Saying?

I grabbed my keys and walked out so I could pick up the soldier assigned to escort me. I was ready for this shit and couldn't wait to show Marcus how to really be a boss.

****

CARRIE

"So, nigga, you are saying that this white bitch here is going to be bringing me product and picking up the money. Yall muthafuckas done lost y'all damn mind," the trapper stated.

Instead of my soldier stepping up to my defense, I stepped up. "The bitch is the one who had you muthafucka. You better check your damn self because I don't mind shooting your ass to get my point across. Now, I'm here to pick up the money so you need to be handing me something, "I stated with a straight-up attitude.

The trapper smiled at me and nodded his head and said, "Damn, that gangsta shit you talkin' turned me the fuck on. What's up girl? You gon' let a nigga hit that before you leave with all my money?"

I couldn't believe that he had the audacity to try me, so, I did what I needed to do. I told the soldier, "Go out there and open the back door to the ride. It seems like I'm gonna have to make an example out of this boy in front of me."

The soldier did as I told him and when I thought he had been outside long enough to open the door, I called out, "Come on in babies, Mama needs you." As soon as I said it, Heyman and Karma came through the door with drool dripping from their mouths.

The trapper's eyes grew large. "Aiight, aiight." he pleaded. "All that ain't called for. I get the message." He went and grabbed a duffel bag from behind the couch and handed it to me.

I said, "Now see, that wasn't so hard, was it? The next time you see my face, I better not have to ask you for shit or I'm gonna start swinging." I nodded my head at my soldier and he dropped the bag full of dope at the trapper's feet. Me and the soldier turned to leave but before I walked out the door, I turned and said, "And it better all be here. If not, I will be back but it will be these two beasts you'll be talking to instead of me." And then, I slammed the door.

****

KRYSTAL

"Damn, Marcus ain't tell us you were that damn pretty. Shit, you can get all this money and mine too. I'm gon' love doing business with your fine ass," the trapper named King said when he opened the door. I could tell that Marcus' trappers didn't have much respect for him because of the comments made to me. However, they did respect the game so they were all straight up, and I wasn't worried about it backfiring.

King's partner, Killa, didn't seem as friendly when he brought out the book bag full of money and dropped it at my feet. He looked me in the eyes and said, "Here's the money. You got the re-up?"

I raised my eyebrows. "Well, hello to you, too, and yeah I got the product for your re-up but you gotta show me some respect. I don't know who the fuck you take me for but I'm not a mutha-fuckin' dog you throw something at and tell to fetch."

"Bitch, who the fuck you think you talking to. Marcus should have told you about me. They don't call me Killa for nothing. You don't come up in my shit like you running things with yo' white ass," Killa exclaimed angrily.

The soldier pulled his weapon and put the tip of the nozzle to Killa's head. "Nigga, watch yo' muthafuckin' mouth. You don't answer to Marcus no more, you answer to her."

"I put a hand on the soldier's arm, saying, "Nah, it ain't gonna go like this. Put your strap away. he's good. Trust me, I complete-ly understand what's going on here." I paused my words for a second and then continued, turning my attention back to Killa. "You think you're gonna bring your ass up in my face and scare me away but that's not going to work on me. I've been bred by the legend that you look up to. Eventually, you either gonna respect me or you gonna respect the bullet that has your name on it. Please don't take me or anything I say lightly because I don't make threats, I make promises. I can assure you, I keep them too." I looked down at my feet where the bookbag lay. "Now, kneel your ass down and pick that bag back up and hand it to me."

I could see his nose as it flared and his mouth twitched show-ing his anger. Neither one of us said a word for a couple of minutes and the only noise in the room was heavy breathing. King finally broke the silence. "Dawg, don't fuck up what we got going on. Shit, I'd rather deal with her pretty ass than Marcus' fucked up face. That nigga knows he is ugly." King laughed at his own joke and I could tell that he would always be the clown at the party. I liked his style and was glad to do business with him.

Me and Killa continued to stare each other down and when he realized that I wasn't backing down, he let out a small chuckle and then bent down and retrieved the bag he had dropped at my feet. I smiled at him when I took the bag. "See, now that's more like it. That hard shit you doing don't phase me. Mark my words, one day we gonna be best friends." I nodded to my soldier to hand him the re-up and turned to leave.

Before I walked all the way out, I heard Killa saying to King, "I like that bitch's style, and she's gonna always have my loyalty." I smiled at his comment because I felt in my heart that his words would always ring true.

****

MARCUS

"Baby, you did real good today. Come here and let a nigga reward ya pretty ass," I said when Krystal came out of the kitchen with a plate full of French fries, her favorite food.

"This plate of homemade fries is the only reward a girl like me needs," she said and plopped down on the opposite end of the couch.

I shook my head. "So, you really ain't gonna give a nigga no pussy. Dick all hard and shit. Come on lil mama." I reached over and put my hand on her bare thigh. The boy shorts she had on left nothing to the imagination. I looked up at her and when she sucked a fry into her mouth, I slid my hand up a little further but before it reached its destination, I heard my cell phone ring. "Damn, it's like a muthafucka know when shit is about to get freaky. Fuck!"

Krystal laughed. "If you answer that, you ain't gonna get none of this pussy so you better let it ring." She opened her thighs and put a hand over her fat print and rubbed. My dick was hard as a rock, but for a nigga like me, who was bred in the streets, business always came before pleasure.

I sat up and picked my phone up from the arm of the couch and answered, "This shit better be good because it just cost me a piece of pussy. Speak your peace."

"Man, this Mirco. Blow and Black just got run in on. Nigga they laid out leaking." Micro's in a voice was panicked. He had always been my weakest soldier.

I stood up from where I sat, forehead wrinkled. "What the fuck man! Anybody talking?"

"Somebody mentioned the name Trigger but dawg I 'don't know who the fuck that is."

Trigger was a little nigga that worked for Temple but why he was aiming his guns at me was a mystery that I needed to solve. "Yo, leave them and I'll call the *cleaners* to go over there. Keep asking around because there's no way Trigger could have pulled that off by himself. Call me if anything else is spoken. I'm out."

I hung up and immediately dialed Temple's number. As soon as he picked up, I stated, "So you sent Trigger at my people? What's the beef you got with me, bro? I thought me and you were good."

"Ain't no beef coming from *me*. Try another source. Our business has been good so why would I send bullets your way? You have a guilty conscience, Marcus? Besides, I have let Trigger go. Lil nigga formed a habit and weak niggas like him will bring down a whole operation."

"Facts. But two of my people just got hit and now I'm wondering what's next? Especially when I don't know who's behind this shit."

"Sounds like you have a problem, family. Unfortunately, it's one I can't assist you with. However, if I hear anything I'll definitely put you up on the move. In the meantime, it sure would be nice to see that package you brought with you last time," Temple said.

I knew that he was talking about Krystal but that would never go down. "Nah, mama off limits. That package belongs only to me and a nigga like me don't share."

He chuckled. "If you change your mind, she's always welcome here," he said, then he hung up.

Even though Temple said he didn't send Trigger my way, I still felt like he knew about the hit on my people. I knew in my gut that there was a war about to begin, one that I wouldn't be able to control. I just hoped that my crew was ready.

****

BLACK

90

I heard the footsteps before anyone knocked on the door but didn't expect to find what I did when I opened it. "Back the fuck up nigga," stated the man with the Mac twelve pointed at me.

I held my hands up to let whoever it was know that there wasn't any beef and that he wouldn't have any problems coming from me. He looked around the front room checking to see if I was alone but my boy, Blow was in the back room getting dicking down the female he'd brought home from the club the night before. I just hoped that the bitch's moans didn't drown out our voices. I needed that muthafucka to get out of the pussy and realize what was going on.

I said loudly, "Aye, dawg, the bread and butter ain't here. I don't shit where I sleep so you are leaving here empty-handed. Why don't you put take that out my face and we can discuss this like two grown muthafuckas."

"What do you think I am, a dumb nigga or something? You think I'm here on a dry run? Nah, I know exactly where the bread and butter are and I'm not leaving here without it."

About that time, the moaning of the broad Blow was fucking seeped through the thin walls, "Shit! Mmm hmm. Yeah Blow, fuck me nigga. Shit, I'm about to cum all over this dick. Yes!"

The gunman looked at me through bloodshot eyes. The sweat on his forehead popped up in little wet bubbles. He put a finger to his lips to tell me to be quiet and then motioned for me to turn around and walk. I knew he wanted me to lead him to the room where the boy and the loud bitch were in but I tried to lead him another way. If nothing else, maybe one of us could make it out of here with our heart still beating.

I felt the butt of the gun when it slammed against my head "Ugh!" I cried out and reached up to grab the spot. The blood covered my hand, the wetness drained down my head and onto my shirt. "Nigga what was that for?" I asked.

"That's for leading me in the wrong direction. Now, I'm gonna give you one more chance to take me where the shit is at. Move muthafucka!" he barked.

Leading him in the wrong direction. His comment told me that this was an inside job. Whoever had sent him had been in the house before and knew the layout well. My mind started to race. *Who the fuck could have sent this beef our way and did Marcus even know about it?* I prayed that I'd live to find out. I had never answered my door without a piece on me and the one time I did, this is what it got me.

"Who the fuck sent you here?" I asked.

"Nigga, I ask the questions if one needs to be asked. Now, open that door, and move carefully when you do. I know about the trap on it so, open that bitch real slowly."

The door to the stash pot was fitted with a trap that only the crew knew about. If the door was opened too fast, laser beams would cross the room and block off the area of the floor the stash was in. Anyone who walked between those beams was met with lines of bullets, quickly ending their existence. The door had to be opened very slowly and precisely to keep the beams at bay.

I started to sweat and continued to pray that Blow would get his nut and walk out of that fucking bedroom because I had a feeling that my ass was history if he didn't. I tried again to stall the perpetrator. "Come on man, put that piece up off of me. A nigga ain't trying to die tonight. You can have all this shit, bruh. It ain't worth my life."

"Yeah, so you want me to submit to yo' ass like I'm some damn fool. I'm just gonna put the gun down and we gon' chop it up like old friends, huh? You a funny as nigga, but I ain't got no sense of humor. Open the fuckin' door or I'ma clap yo' ass right here, right now!"

"A'ight. Just be easy, fam." I went ahead and opened the door, slowly.

The gunman shoved me forward. "Thanks young G but yo' services are no longer needed."

"Wait! Wait man! Don't you need me to show you where it is?"I asked although I knew that he had already been given that information. However, I was trying to do what I could to stay alive a little longer. I couldn't believe that Blow had not heard any of what was going on right outside his door. I was pissed that he was so into the pussy that he didn't even realize I was in jeopardy, but I need that nigga to pull out so I hollered like a bitch. "Blow! Blow, help me! We getting robbed. Blow, he...." Everything went black.

****

BLOW

"Hell no. Nigga, where the fuck are you going? You ain't done with this pussy. I wanna feel you inside me again," Tina said as she grabbed at my dick.

I slapped her hand away. "Bitch shut the fuck up. Something is wrong. Stay here and be as quiet as you can. If I don't make it back, call Micro and get outta here as fast as you can." I slid on a pair of Nike sweats and grabbed my gun from the drawer. I crept out of the bedroom and shut the door behind me. Tina was a smart bitch so I knew she would follow my instructions.

Tina was my homeboy Micro's little sister but he didn't know we had been fucking ever since she turned eighteen. However, if something happened to me, he would soon find out. I had been so deep in the pussy that I almost didn't hear Black calling out to me. He sounded like he was in duress so I pulled out and went to see what was wrong. I walked through our house slowly and as quietly as I could but didn't see Black anywhere, and then, I felt something hard hit me in the back of the head.

"Muthafucka, you should have stayed in the pussy and you would have lived," I heard the man say when I dropped to my knees.

His voice sounded familiar but it took a minute before my eyes would focus and when I finally saw his face, I asked, "Trigger? Nigga, what's going on? What the fuck are you doing?"

Trigger and I had grown up in the same neighborhood. We both ended up in an Augusta Detention Center at the same time. We had formed a close bond at one time but when he hooked up with Temple, I went another way. I didn't fuck with Temple because word on the street was that he liked to take pussy and I didn't fuck with niggas who violated women. I respected women too much for that and ended up with Marcus instead. However, I couldn't understand why Trigger was doing this shit.

"Shut the fuck up. You already know that you ain't gonna make it outta here so say your last prayer because it's over for you." He stuck the gun up under my chin. "You'll find your friend Black in hell. He will be waiting for you there."

"Wait, wait! Who sent you? Just tell me that before you kill me. I deserve that much," I said.

He laughed and placed the barrel of the gun to the middle of my chest and said one name before he pulled the trigger.

****

MICRO

When I saw my little sister's number pop up on the screen followed by a 911, I answered immediately. "Aye, where are you at. You aiight, sis?"

"Terrance. Oh my God.! It's Blow and his boy. They... they... Oh my God.! Terrance, I think they're dead. He killed them!"

I knew I heard her right but still couldn't believe what she'd said. "Wait, sis. Calm down. What happened to Blow and Black? Where the fuck you at?"

"He killed them. And he knew I was there so he's probably looking for me now. Oh my god what am I gonna do? Terrance, you gotta come get me. I know he's still there. Please save me," she cried out.

"Tina, where are you and who the hell are you talking about? Who killed Blow and Black? Talk to me. Tell me where you are so I can come get you." I kept my voice calm, hoping to calm her down a bit.

"Blow called him *Trigger*. I'm at his house under the back porch, but I'm scared. I know... I know... oh my god, shh, shhh, shh," she cried, and then suddenly she went quiet.

"Sis, try to be as still as you can. I'm on my way." I started to end the call but thought better of it. "Don't hang this phone up no matter what. Stay on the line and be as quiet as you can. Do that for me, okay. I got you."

I had known for the longest time that Blow and my little sister were fucking but I never said shit because Blow was a good nigga. I sped as fast as I could to get to Tina. She was my fucking heart and I would never be able to live with myself if something happened to her. I was trying to figure out why someone would hit Blow and Black. They had never caused no beef in the streets, which probably meant the shooter was sending a message to someone else.

As soon as I pulled up to the house, I pulled out my gun and had it ready just in case I had to split a nigga's wig. I could faintly hear Tina still crying on the phone. "Okay, sis, I'm out front but I don't see anybody. Where you at?"

She replied, "I'm around back, under the porch. I think he gave up and left, but Terrance I'm scared to move."

The fear in her voice broke my heart because my little sis should never have to fear anything as long as I had breath in my lungs. I spoke as calmly as I could. "Okay, just stay where you are. I'm gonna check the house and make sure you're clear. I'm putting my phone in my pocket so you can still hear me. If you happen to see him, let me know, your voice will come through on my ear piece. You understand?"

"Yes. Please, be careful Terrance."

"Don't worry, sis, I'm good."

I opened the front door and crept inside slowly. I didn't see anyone so I went in further. I checked the kitchen and still nothing. I started down the hall and that's when I saw a foot sticking out from the door of the stash room, but before I went in there, I checked Blow's bedroom.

I finally turned back around to head to the stash room and noticed the foot had disappeared. I moved slower to the door and when I got there, I wasn't prepared for what I saw. Black's head was split open and brain matter was all over the wall. I turned and looked at Blow who was leaning against the chair and looked to still be alive. I walked over and put a hand to his neck feeling for a pulse. He suddenly lifted his head and scared the shit out of me.

"Blow, hold on my nigga, I'm gonna get you out of here. Shit." I looked around for a sheet or something that I could wrap around him and then drag him out. I faintly heard him as he tried to speak so, I turned back to him and put my ear to his mouth. "Speak to me, dawg. Speak to me so I know you are still good."

He shook his head and coughed out, "Trigger. He sent Trigger."

"I didn't know who Trigger was or who he was talking about sent him, so I asked, "Who the fuck is Trigger B? Who are you talking about sent him? Tell me something man."

"Your sister, I-I ugh. Ugh, your sis…" he said and reminded me that she was still on the line. I had totally forgotten that she was still hiding under the house. The scene I walked up on made me turn my focus. I finally said, "Tina, sis, you can come out. Come in the house, Blow is still alive. We gotta get him to the hospital or he ain't gonna make it."

I heard when she cried out, "Oh my God. Nooo! Not Blow."

"Aiight dawg, I'm gonna grab a sheet and wrap it around you so I can drag you outta here. Don't move shit you ain't gotta move. Okay" I said in a calm voice so he wouldn't panic.

About that time, Tina came through the door and ran straight to Blow. She knelt down and started to kiss his face and said, "Oh my God, baby hold on. Please hold on, please don't leave me. Please Hurry up, Terrance."

Blow reached up with a bloody hand and touched Tina's face. She put her hand over his and as the tears fell down her beautiful face, she said, "Baby, I love you so much. Please hold on, I need you. We got a whole life ahead of us. Please."

My heart broke more and more with each tear she shed. Their love for each other was genuine, so genuine that even a blind man could see it. I found a sheet and walked over to them and said, "Come on sis, lean him over on this sheet so we can get him out of here."

Blow shook his head and said, "Nah, this is it for me man. I ain't gonna make it outta here. You go and avenge me and my nigga over there. Just go. Shit hurts like a muthafucka but ain't nothin' you can do. This it is."He then looked Tina in the eyes and said, "I ain't never seen a female that meant more to me than you. Girl, you changed a nigga's heat and made it beat steady. Carry on with life baby girl and make a nigga respect you. Don't ever settle for anything less. You hear me? A nigga loves yo' ass and even though, another won't ever love you as much as me. Don't be afraid to let them love you with all they got. You are mine forever boo. Don't ever forget that okay. A nigga gonna be waiting on you when you get there okay."His tears singed my insides and made my eyes sting with some of their own.

Blow began coughing violently and with each one blood poured out from his chest. I knew in my heart that even if we would have taken him to the hospital, he wouldn't have made it. His wound was deep and he'd already lost a lot of blood. He looked at me one final time and said, "You check them niggas before you let them fuck with her. I'm sorry dawg, we should have told you but I ain't know how you would act. Please forgive me, man. Go get that muthafucka that sent Trigger our way and make his ass pay, put Marcus up on that shit okay."

I nodded my head and questioned Blow. "Yo, man, who sent him? You never told me that."

Blow opened his mouth to speak but before he got out the name, his eyes closed for good.

Corey Robinson

Chapter Nine
FEELOW

"So, I'm not understanding. If y'all made a truce, why are you breaking it again, Feelow. I thought you'd be happy that you could finally get back right," Keisha stated and looked at me like I had lost my mind.

I replied, "Yeah, I thought we had made a truce and then that muthafucka told me that this white bitch he has been fucking was gonna take shit over. Hell no, ain't no damn white girl filling my void! Fuck him and her pale ass."

Keisha lifted an eyebrow and said, "A white girl. Nigga, you are tripping. Marcus ain't that damn stupid. Besides, I never heard him speak of a white bitch. Where the hell did she come from?"

"She was walking through the block one day and Marcus saw her and we did the usual but I guess he saw something special in her because that nigga been keeping house with her ass."I responded and then said, "You sure asking a lot of damn questions. Your ass better not be keeping tabs and shit for that nigga."

"Really, Feelow. I ain't gon' lie, I'm appreciative of him because he got me off the street and honestly, I think he saved me and my baby. I don't know if I would have made it this far with our son without him. I feel like I owe him some sort of loyalty," she said.

"Bitch, you are in here praising that nigga in my muthafucking Face. Have you lost your fuckin mind? That's my seed growing inside of you so watch yo' mouth. You are lucky he is in there because right now, I wanna beat your ass for saying that shit. Stupid ass, "I stated angrily. I just couldn't believe that Keisha would take up for that nigga right in my face after knowing that me and Marcus had a beef. I laid back on the bed and said, "Come over here and put this dick in your mouth. Gotta do something to stop that reckless talking."

"Nigga, fuck you and fuck me and you. I don't need your black ass and neither does this baby. I'm outta this bitch," she said while she gathered the few things she owned. I jumped up from the bed and grabbed her by the arm to stop her. I knew I had to kiss her ass at least until my seed was born and then, her dumb ass would be history.

When she turned to face me, I put on the charm and said, "Ah come on baby. You know a nigga just feeling some type of way about that muthafucka. I just don't like to hear my bitch praise the next man. Shit, a nigga wants all this to himself. Damn girl, I apologize. Now, come on and let me get some of my pussy."

The smile that showed up on her face let me know that I was off the hook. She said, "Okay but be gentle because you could hurt Khalif with all that dick you're gonna be pushing up in there."

We shared a laugh and when I bent over to kiss her, my phone rang. "No Fellow, don't answer that," she pleaded but when I saw who the caller was, I knew I had no choice. The voice came through from the other side as soon as I hit accept. "Checkmate," he said and hung up.

****

KEISHA

As soon as Feelow left, I picked up the phone to call Marcus. He had been so good to me and my baby for those few months so I at least wanted him to know that we were okay. However, I was very surprised that he answered on the first ring, "What the fuck you want Keisha? I got business to tend to right now so this shit better be good" He said into the phone in a voice that made me feel like shit. I knew that he was disappointed at my choice to go back to Feelow but what else was I supposed to do. Feelow was my baby's father and he would need him when he was born. I had grown up without one and I didn't want my son to suffer the same fate.

I replied. "Damn, Marcus, why are you acting like that? I just wanted to call and let you know that I'm okay. What the fuck?"

"Keisha, a nigga like me don't have time for your bullshit. I helped you because I thought you wanted a better life but now, I see that I was wrong," He exclaimed angrily.

100

"Marcus, Feelow is ready for fatherhood. He's not going to do anything crazy. He loves me and besides, I thought y'all made up. What happened?"I asked curiously. How did things between them turn back sour so quickly?

"Look let me be the first to tell you that the muthafucka doesn't give a damn about you, Keisha. If you were having a girl, he would have left yo' ass but knowing that you have a son that can carry on his legacy, keeps him around," he pauses as if he thought about his next words carefully. "Keisha, when you have his son, he is going to dispose of you. He doesn't want yo' ass. That nigga likes dick too much to keep you around. You gotta get away from him."

"Fuck you, Marcus, your ass is just mad that you can't run me. What were you gonna do, pass my son off as yours or something? You invested a lot of time and money into a child that doesn't even belong to you. I ain't going nowhere so don't worry about me. As a matter of fact, worry about the white bitch you put in my man's spot," I stated with attitude and hung up.

I threw my phone down on the bed and then wondered how much of what Marcus had told me was true. Why would Feelow want to eliminate me after I gave birth? I felt kinda bad about the way I had done Marcus but there was nothing I could do about that. However, I decided to be safe rather than sorry and packed my things. I wasn't going to stick around to see if Marcus' words rang true. I hoped that I was doing the right thing when I walked out of the small apartment and away from Feelow.

I had to hurry because as soon as he got back and realized I was gone, my life would be in jeopardy.

****

FEELOW

"Nigga what took you so fuckin' long?"Trigger asked as soon as he opened the door to the room he had hidden out in.

"Bitch, you answer to me not the other way around," I said angrily and walked in. I looked around the room and noticed the pile of bloody clothes and said, "Hey, you crazy muthafucka man. You gotta burn that shit. Have you lost yo' damn mind?"

"Yeah, I plan on taking care of that and I'm gon' relocate to another motel for awhile," Trigger stated and pulled out his pipe. He looked up at me before he pinched a piece of the dope off and put it on the brillo-filled glass. He asked, "You, you want a hit of this shit or something/your ass watching me might be hard."

My nose flared because I was feigning for a hit, however, I wasn't about to let him know it. I said, "Nah nigga, I'm here to pick up my shit. The fuck yo' mind at?"

He struck the lighter and melted his rock on the brillo. The sizzle of the drug caused my stomach to bubble. I turned my head for a brief second so the feeling would pass. Before Trigger put the pipe into his mouth, he said, "It's all in that closet over there, and don't forget to give me my share. I know what's there so don't try to cheat my ass."

I got up and opened the closet door to find four black duffle bags. Two were filled with cash and the other two with Kilos of cocaine and cookies of crack. There had to be at least a hundred and fifty G's in each bag. I smiled at the find. I had always known that Blow and Black made the most of all Marcus Trap boys but didn't expect it to be like that. My mouth watered when I picked up the cookies and couldn't wait to leave there so I could enjoy the treasure I held. I picked up the four bags and turned around. Trigger had gotten fully undressed and was peeking out the motel room window with his gun in his hand. I said, "Nigga, you are tripping. Put that shit down and close those blinds before your ass gets noticed. The fuck is wrong wit' you?"

I wasn't ready for the answer he gave me."Man, Blow recognized me. We grew up in foster homes together and shit. That shit is fucking with me man, really bad."

"Why the fuck you worried, that nigga is in the dust now so, your name ain't even gonna be mentioned. Just chill man," I said and counted out fifty thousand dollars along with a key of cocaine and two cookies. I threw them on the bed and zipped the bags back up. I picked them up and started to leave but his words stopped me in my tracks. "Someone else was there."

I looked him in the eyes and asked, "What the fuck did you just say? Nigga, who was there? You got 'em right."When he held his head down, I knew what his answer would be. He stated, "Nah, she must have run or hidden where I couldn't find her. I looked everywhere, dawg but that bitch was gone."

"What? Nigga who was it? Did she know you?"I asked anxiously.

"Nah, I don't even think she saw me. But Blow said my name out loud so she may be able to tell Marcus who I am. Nigga, I don't know what to do," he stated and walked back over to the bed and sat down.

I couldn't take a chance at having a loose end. If Marcus came for him, he would torture him until he talked. I had to take care of the issue myself so, I put the duffle bags down and said, "You know what, I think I do want a hit of that shit. Why don't you fill that pipe up for me? Put a big piece on there, enough to clear my head."

He looked at me funny but did as I told him. When he passed the stem to me, I lit the end and inhaled hard, filling my lungs with the greatest pleasure I knew. When I blew the smoke out, I passed the stem back to him and undid my jeans, and said, "Aye, won't you come on over here and make a nigga feel good."

Trigger scrunched his face up and said, "Nah Dawg, I don't get down like that. I like to be naked when I get high but that doesn't mean I do shit like you are asking muthafucka, I like pussy."

"Oh yeah? Well today you like dick too, bitch."

I stood up and got in front of him and then pulled my gun out. "Nigga, I ain't asking. You gonna suck this muthafucka until I tell you to stop. Now get busy." I put the tip of the nozzle to his head and he slowly reached up and put a hand around my dick. I kept my gun at his head while he brought me to the edge of an orgasm. I said, "Aiight, listen real good. You should never leave a witness behind, you dumb muthafucka. Now, because you were careless,

I'm gon' have to shut you up."I got quiet while I shot off in his mouth and when I was finished, I pushed him back and put a bullet between his eyes.

****

DITTO

The knock on the door startled me although I was expecting it. When I opened it, Blackout stood there with a smile on his face. He pulled me in for a brotherly hug and said," Damn D, a nigga happy to see you Dawg."

"Yeah, man, it's good to see a familiar face. Come on in,' I said and noticed that he had come alone so I asked, "Aye where ya bitch at man? I asked you to bring her."

"I can't bring a bitch I don't trust man. You know what I'm saying. What'd you need her for anyway?" he asked.

I replied," I had to kill that bitch that hooked me up. She knew too much and she was loyal to the muthafuka I'm gonna snake. Clean up came and took her away though. I just needed a female voice for when those niggas call. Shit, I don't know what I'm gon do now."

"Fuck it man, I got your back," He said and then said something that took me by surprise. "Aye, two of Marcus trappers got lit up last night. Word around town saying a Lil nigga named trigger did it. Took everything they had in there."

"Oh yeah, that's a good thing because when I light more of his Trappers up, he will never suspect me. Does anyone know I'm still alive?"I asked.

Blackout said, "Man, muthafuckas speculate but you know ain't nobody got no concrete. That Lil nigga, Paris is looking in the daylight with a flashlight for that shit you did to his girl and his seed. That was some foul-ass shit man but niggas in the game know the consequences."

"I owed that bastard and his fuckin' daddy. Niggas had that dog almost bite my dick off man. I had to get the head of my shit sewed back on. You should see the way a bitch looks at my dick now.

"I get pissed off every time I pull that muthafucka out," I stated. Although, I had gone to a plastic surgeon to fix my dick, that shit still didn't look right. If that dog would have bit any harder, ~~I would have bit any harder,~~ I would have been made into a bitch. Paris and Stone had to pay for that shit.

Blackout asked, "So what's the plan now, boss man? I'm ready to do whatever you say. It's time to take yo' shit back so what's up?"

"Chill homie, I don't want to rush into anything. Did you bring me the money I asked for?"I asked.

He replied, "Yeah man, it's a bag in the trunk of the rental car. It's still warm too."

Blackout was a master at making counterfeit money and no one was the wiser. I had paid all of my connections with it over the years and was about to do the same with Stanley Earl, especially since the next pick-up would be done by an underling. After I got the work, I would flee and hide out until Blackout could send a hitman to eliminate the problem. By the time Stan figured out the money was fake; his ass would be six feet deep.

Blackout asked, "Yo' man, you sure that nigga ain't gonna be able to tell that shit ain't right? I think I've heard his name out here in the streets and from what I heard, bro ain't lame at all."

"Man, that muthafucka dumb as fuck. He won't to catch on to g this shit. Besides, he ain't doing the pick-up. He was supposed to send an amateur so that's on him," I said. If my ultimate plan didn't work, I would blame it on the nigga he sent.

****

TYCK

"So, you want me to make sure it's the ether cut that he smokes instead of the good shit?" I asked Toe Tag who wanted me to make the switch on the cocaine. I wasn't sure about the move because I didn't want Feelow's blood on my hands.

Toe Tag said, "You're his boy so, he trusts you. All you do is help him with the cooking and packaging like you always do and fix his ass up a big hit. Light that bitch for him if you have to. I don't give a fuck. Just get it done. That nigga gonna lose his muthafucking mind. I want his ass to suffer."

I asked, "What if it doesn't kill him and he figures out that I switched that shit? Then what?"

"Look, that nigga is gonna start hallucinating and shit. You'll know when it's time to jet so get yo' ass outta there when you see him change up. You gon' be able to handle this shit or do I gotta find someone else to do it?"Toe Tag stated.

"Nah, I got it. I can handle it. Don't worry. You just get the shit and make sure, I know which one is the lace," I said nervously. I hoped that I could pull this off because if I didn't succeed, it could very well mean my life.

****

PARIS

"Aye man, I'm glad you made it in time. I thought you had changed your mind or something," Thomas said when he opened the door to his lush condo.

I replied, "Changed my mind. Nigga, I have been dreaming about this shit. I can't wait to break that muthafucka's neck."

"That's what I'm talking about. Let's get the party started," Stanley Earl stated when he walked into the room with a female and introduced her to me. "This here is Layla and she's going to make that ride with you."

"Hell no. I don't need any distractions." I looked the cocoa-colored female down and knew that if I took her with me, she would distract me from the mission. She was beautiful and the first woman I had found myself attracted to since Torrie's murder. I instantly became consumed with guilt. I stated, "I don't think it is a good idea to take her. Why can't you send a soldier with me, instead?"

106

Stanley Earl laughed. "Layla is a soldier although a very beautiful one. Don't let her beauty confuse you. Layla is lethal as hell. I can assure you she will have your back at all costs. Besides, I want her to handle Sarah just in case she feels the need to be loyal to that piece of shit."

"Yo man, Layla is certified and can shoot with the best of them. First, her beauty blinds them and then, the rest is history. A muthafucka will never see her coming," Thomas said as a matter of fact.

"Yeah, she built like that?" I stated and when she walked up on me, my dick instantly stood at attention. I had not touched another woman since Torrie. I couldn't bring myself to move on, at least not until I avenged her death. I know that she wouldn't want me to live my life lonely but without torrie. I wasn't sure I still wanted to live. However, the presence of Layla seemed to bring my senses back to life.

She finally spoke. "Yes, I am built for that. Don't let these heels fool you. I can run with the best of them. I just hope that you can keep up."

Her boldness made her even sexier. "Keep up?" I chuckled. "A nigga like me already started without you. Don't get left behind." Her smile melted my insides but I wasn't ready at least not until Ditto stopped breathing.

Stanley Earl broke the vibe in the room. "The nigga called a little while ago and said that he had my money and was ready for the re-up but that muthafucka ain't even been nowhere to sell that still so, I know he is lying. I got a man keeping watch and he said another man showed up with a couple of bags but he didn't know who he was."

Thomas asked, "Yeah, can you think of anyone he could call on and bring into this? We need to know what to prepare for.

I thought for a minute and then said, "The only Lil nigga that still rides for him is Blackout. You gotta be careful with your money when he's around. Nigga is known for drawing up fake bills and passing them. That could explain how he came up with the money that quick. Didn't you say you got a female in there too?"

"Yeah, but I feel in my gut that something happened to her. I was blowing up her phone. Even got her cousin, Heather, to call her but the bitch ain't responding. That shit is off man. Sarah's the one that hooked him up but she would never ignore my calls. Plus, I feel like she wouldn't let me do anything that's not right, but the dick could also have blinded her."

About that time, Thomas's phone buzzed and he answered and listened to the caller, he hung up he said, "It's show time.

****

DITTO

"Man what if that nigga asks about that bitch you made disappear? He might be suspicious if she ain't around," Blackout asked.

"Nah, he ain't even gonna have time to ask about her. We're gonna make this deal quick. In and out. I don't even want him in here long enough to think about her ass. Shit, nigga shouldn't be asking about my bitch no way. Fuck him." I peeked out of the blinds to make sure I didn't see anything unusual.

It felt like I had been waiting for hours when finally heard a knock finally at the door. I looked at Blackout who then pulled out his pistol and made sure it was locked and ready. He stood to the side and when I looked through the peephole, I didn't expect what I'd seen. I motioned for Blackout to relax so he put his gun away but continued to stay close. I opened the door and the woman on the other side said, "Stanley Earl sent me. I brought you what you've asked for so are you gonna let me in or not?" Stanley Earl had to be the dumbest muthafukca on the planet to send a woman to do his work. I knew that because of his dumb mistake that everything I had planned would go in my favor. I opened the door wider and let her in and then looked outside to make sure there were no unexpected visitors with her. She noticed and asked, "Are you expecting someone else? Because you can't possibly be checking behind me."

I shut the door and said, "Nah, a nigga just making sure no one followed you. That's all."

"Oh yeah, don't worry. No one is dumb enough to follow me. I'm not new to this shit so, let's handle what I came for so I can be on my way," she said in a demanding voice.

I nodded to Blackout and he picked up the bag that contained the counterfeit bills and dropped it on the table in front of the woman who never revealed her name. I asked, "So, what's your name sweetheart?"

She unzipped the bag to check the money and looked up at me and stated, "First of all, it is not sweetheart and honestly, names aren't really that important are they? This is only business so, all that matters is that the money and product are right."

"Yeah, okay let's get down to business then. When are you going to hand me the product? I've put the money in front of you but you've made no effort to give me that bag you brought in with you," I said and then, Blackout cut in, "Yeah, what's up with that? You are making a nigga feel like some funny shit is going on so why don't you hand over what we are paying for?"

She zipped the bag back up and said, "How about I hand it over when you pay me in real money and not this fuckin monopoly shit you have in this bag."

I looked at Blackout and then back at the female who said, "What? You thought you were gonna get over because I'm a woman or were you thinking Stanley Earl wouldn't notice?"

Blackout said, "Nah, Lil mama you are mistaken. Ain't no way that money ain't real. You fuckin trippin' and shit. That green is legit."

"Thanks alright, I'll call Stanley Earl myself and let him know that he should have never sent a woman to do a man's job. Your dumb ass can't even tell real money from fake money. Feel like you are trying to get a nigga hemmed up and shit." I pulled out my phone to call Stanley Earl and when he picked up, I said, "Yo, why you send in a bitch to do this deal. This muthafucker doesn't know what the fuck she is talking about? You need to get over here."

"I'm busy but don't worry, I've sent someone else to help you out."

I was confused because he sounded as if he already knew the deal. "What was going on before I called. What the fuck do you mean you sent someone else? This bitch came by herself."

"Open the front door," he replied and hung up.

I motioned for Blackout to watch the female while I went to the door. When I looked out the peephole, I didn't see anybody. I went against my better judgment and opened it to look around outside and when I did, I ran into a blast from my past. One I hoped to never see again. The gun was pointed at my head when he said, "What's up nigga. Happy to see me?"

I held my hands up and began to back up slowly, "Paris. How did you know where to find me?"I asked and hoped that Blackout had heard me, but Paris was well aware of his surroundings. He kept his gun pointed at me all the way to the living room and that's when I noticed Blackout sprawled out on the floor with a hole in his throat.

The female turned her gun to me. "That money is fake but the bullet your man swallowed was real. You good Paris?"

Paris smiled at her and said, "Yeah, Layla. Thanks. Grab all those bags and check the apartment to see if there's anything else in here and then go wait for me in the car."

The female did as he said and while I waited for an opportunity to jump, I knew that I wouldn't find one. I had to pay for the things I'd done to Paris whether I wanted to or not.

I laughed and said, "Bitch pretty and gangsta as fuck but she could never replace Torrie. Huh nigga? That pussy was as good as the one that carried your bastard? Huh, you Lil muthafucka? Go ahead and kill me, I don't give a fuck no more. I lived a good life. It's you that's living a miserable one. Where's your fuck ass daddy. Huh? Where is he, a little orphan boy? Ha! Ha! Ha!"

At that time, Stone walked into the room and asked, "You looking for me, Ditto? Nigga, you knew I couldn't have been too far away. There's no way I would miss the opportunity to see your muthafucking brain explode. Too bad I don't have time to make popcorn. Go ahead, son, I'm just gonna sit back and take a load off while you handle this bitch."

Stone sat on the couch and propped his feet up and Paris said, "Nigga, this is for my momma." He then fired a bullet into my left knee.

"Shit! Fuck you, muthafucka. She was my bitch. She should have stayed in her place. Ha! Ha! That bitch could suck a mean dick," I cried out and held on to my knee.

Paris said, "This is for my wife. Nigga, you took her with no remorse when she ain't do shit to nobody."

Pow! He blasted be in my right kneecap.

Covering the wound with both hands and grimacing, I gritted, "Yeah, I should have kidnapped that bitch and showed her what a real man is, but you were selfish with that pussy. Unlike Daddy-O, who left his bitch for me when he went to prison? I should have cut that bastard right out of her stomach and raised him as mine. At least, he could have had a real man in his life."

Stone raised his eyebrows. "Nigga, you thought we weren't gonna come back for you and avenge our people? You deserve every bullet that's in that clip. As a matter of fact, son, let me assist you with this last shot." He stood from the couch and pulled out his own gun. Both of them stood over me and aimed their guns at my head.

Paris said, "Nah, pops, you kill the mind and I'll take care of his heart."

He lowered his gun to my chest and spat, "Nigga, this is for my seed, the one that I'll never meet because of you."

"Fuck you, muthafucka!" I cried out, ready for them to get it over with.

Paris said one last thing. "Oh yeah, Marcus sends his love, bitch."And then, they both pulled the trigger.

****

PARIS

I couldn't believe that I had finally gotten the opportunity to avenge Torre's death. I knew that I could now finally move on with my life. I called Thomas.

"I'm done man. I'm getting outta this life. Thanks for your help."

"No problem, man. You know you my nigga. Do you need anything else?" Thomas asked.

I looked over at Layla and then back at my pops and knew that I had everything I needed. I said, "Nah, I'm good. We are about to swing by and drop off y'all's shit and then, I'm gon' take Layla with me. I feel like Torrie would be okay with that."

Thomas replied, "Yeah dawg. She is a good person and I hope she can fill that void. I'll see you when you get here."

I hung up the phone and looked up to the sky and before I drove away, I sent a word to Torrie," Checkmate baby. Rest In Peace"

Chapter Ten
KRYSTAL

"Damn girl, who lives in that mansion. That shit is nice as hell," Carrie said as soon as I pulled up in Brandon's driveway. If I didn't know better, I would swear that a real-life movie star lived there, instead of a drug dealer. He had done his thing and invested his money wisely.

I said, "Act like you've been to a place like this before because you'll be coming here more often. I don't want B-Line to think that I'm bringing a rookie to take my spot."I gathered my purse and pulled the keys out of the ignition and looked up into the face of the only threat Marcus had.

Carrie noticed it. "I've never seen you look like that before. You're in love with whoever he is, aren't you?"

"His name is B-Line and yes, Carrie, I am quite smitten by him but my heart belongs to Marcus. Forget what you saw. Let's get out and handle this business, "I said and opened my door to get out. Before my feet hit the ground, Brandon was in front of me. So close I could feel his breath as it blew upon me. I regained my composure and said, "I've brought the new mule. She will be taking my place because I've got other tasks to take care of now."

Brandon replied, "Yeah, I heard you were down there being a boss bitch and shit. So that nigga is putting you out in the pack of wolves now. Guess that's where he feels his woman is supposed to be."

"It was my choice, Brandon, I forced his hand," I said and brushed by him. Carrie stood off the side and listened to our exchange. I wondered how much of it she would tell Marcus or even creep, so that he would tell him. I knew if Marcus found out how close, Brandon and I had really gotten, he would shut the shit down quickly. I had to protect Brandon at all costs so I was doing what was best.

"Yeah, let me guess. You caught him with another bitch so you gave him an ultimatum. Put you out in the action with him or you leave," he said and looked at me for an answer but he wasn't getting what he wanted.

"Look after this trip; you won't have to worry about me anymore. You can fuck the new mule instead and let my man worry about me. I'm here on business so, let's go inside and handle it so I can get back on the road," I said with a regretful attitude. That was not how I wanted to end things with him but it was how it turned out.

I left him where he stood and went to the secret compartment of the vehicle. Carrie came and helped me pull out the bags of money and carry them inside. Jambo met us at the door while Brandon follows us from behind.

Brandon came closer to them and whispered in my ear, "You didn't know that your so-called man is in a street beef and the only reason he agreed to put you out there was so that you could get that bullet with his name on it," and then, he left me standing there with those thoughts in my mind.

****

ECHO

"So, it's all set up with Tyck. He is gonna make sure that nigga smokes off the right brick. Muthafucka even gonna fix it up for him. I can't wait to hear about that bastard losing his damn mind," Toe Tag said with a smile.

"Swag, what are you people saying about that shipment? I'm ready to set shit up, plus, I know Feelow got to be out of product soon. I want to have that ready for him," I stated.

Swag T replied, "I talked to Drake about two hours ago and he said they were sending it down by a bitch named Tracy, she should be pulling in soon."About twenty minutes later, the vehicle that pulled up had us all anxious. We all looked forward to the outcome of the situation. I opened the door for the female because I would be the one she'd ask for and when the honey stepped out of the ride, I almost lost all composure. The bitch looked like she was ordered to deliver trash. I had never seen a mule look so ragged out. The vehicle she rode in looked to be just as torn up as she was.

When Tracy got to the door, she said, "Please don't let this fool you. I can assure you, it's all for show. Now, could you please point me in the direction of the nearest bathroom so I can clean up before we do business?"

"Uh, yeah. Come on, I'll show you where it's at." I led her to the back where she could clean up. When she shut the door behind her, I walked away and went back to the living room where Swag and Toe Tag waited.

I looked at Swag. "Bitch, you need to call yo' people and ask them why they sent a muthafucking scrub. Nigga, mules ain't supposed to look like that. Drake done tried yo ass. Bitch look like she done smoked a whole kilo."Man, I don't know what the fuck Drake was thinking but I'm about to cuss his Haitian ass out. Muthafucka done tried us and shit," Swag stated and picked up her phone to dial.

Before she had a chance to even say hello, Tracy appeared before us, looking like a totally different person. She put her hands on her hips and said, "Okay, boys, oh and girl. Shall we get down to business?"

"Holy shit. Are you the same bitch that went into that bathroom," I said and looked at Swag and smiled.

Swag ended his phone call and replied, "Nah, Echo, my people sent her, so that means that I—"

Tracy cut her off, "That doesn't mean shit. Besides, I like dicks so, ain't gonna happen. Let's get this over with so I can get back on the road. Drake doesn't send me on these trips to mingle. Echo, could you follow me outside to collect the product?"

I replied, "Hell yeah. Shit, I'll follow you anywhere you wanna go."

We walked outside to the clunker that she had driven down and she told me to remove the rear tire rims. I did as she said and found three kilos in each tire. The kilos seemed smaller but when I put them on the scale, they weighted perfectly. About thirty minutes later, a silver Lexus pulled up. Tracy said, "Well, that's my ride back. Who knows, maybe next time I could stay a while and Echo could show me around town." She passed the keys to the clunker to the rental driver and got in the Lexus and drove away.

****

MARCUS

"Nigga, where my bitch at?" Feelow asked as soon as I answered the phone.

"I don't know my man, maybe she realized what a piece of shit you are. You should've stuck to dick and you wouldn't be having these problems," I said with a smile on my face. My heart sped up from the hurt that it was experiencing. I couldn't believe that Feelow and I had made up only to fall out again.

"Why stick to one thing when I can have the best of both worlds. What you thought you were gonna do with my seed? Huh? That nigga belongs to me and ain't nobody else gonna be playing daddy to mine. I think I've told you that before, so why don't you go ahead and send Keisha back to me and we'll let it all end there. No more beef, no more drama," Feelow exclaimed.

"Sorry, Fee, but I told you that yo' bitch ain't wit me. I don't gotta lie to you, my brother," I stated.

"Nah, nigga. I ain't yo' brother no more. You forget that you dissed me for a white bitch? You fucking bastard? I'm gon' make that bitch suck my dick and then boom, watch her mouth explode," Feelow said, and I knew he was capable of doing exactly that.

Just the thought of him bringing harm to Krystal had my nose flared. "Nigga, the beef is between us so let's keep it that way."

He laughed. "Between us? You should think about that when you hid my bitch out so I couldn't get to her. So now, that makes your bitch fair game. Better keep an eye on her, Marcus. Never know who could be lurking in the dark."

He hung up.

****

116

B-LINE

"Nigga, let me find out you really feeling that girl there," I said to Jambo who had just come in from a shopping trip with Carrie. She was the first female I had seen him spend any time with in a long time. All the other bitches he fooled with never got more than a hard dick and a few dollars from him so I was happy that maybe he could build something with her.

He replied, "Nah man, it ain't like that. I mean yeah, I'm feeling her energy but she got a nigga already."

"Yeah and I've never seen you give up on something that you wanted so I know you ain't gonna let another man stand in your way," I stated as Krystal walked up and said, "We're leaving in about an hour so could you make sure the truck is packed in for the trip?"

I shook my head. "Nah, baby, you and yo' friend ain't going nowhere for a while. So, chill and enjoy the time we got."

She put her hands on her hips and replied with an attitude, "Fuck you Brandon but I can't stay here and do this with you. I have to get back home to my real man. I'm sorry but you know I can't leave him even if I wanted to."

I was pissed at her response but I let it slide. Had she been any other woman, she would have been on the floor with a bloody nose. But because she was the owner of my heart, I ignored her attitude. I grabbed her arm and pulled her face to face with me. "He's the one who told me to keep you here. He has some shit going on and believe it or not doesn't want you in it. Maybe his ass really does care about you."

She yanked her arm out of my grasp and said, "His beef is mine and I'm walking out of this house today so make sure the truck is packed and ready."

I shook my head. "Are you fucking crazy, Krys? Huh? You're gonna fuck around and get yourself killed. Is that what you want?"

"Not being able to be with you like I want is going to kill me anyway. So, I might as well go ahead and put myself into the line of fire. It's for the best, Brandon. I'm sorry," she said, and then she turned around and walked away.

Carrie and Jambo looked at each other and then at me. I shrugged my shoulders and said to Carrie, "If shit doesn't feel right, you call Jambo immediately. If that bastard even thinks about sending any harm her way, I'll kill him myself." I went to pack the truck.

I felt Krystal's presence before she got to me. When she was close enough, she said, "I thought you said he told you to make me stay until the beef was over."

I held my head down and stood up to face her. "I lied. I thought that if I told you he asked you to stay that you would listen. I'm sorry. I'm just. I just wanted to keep you safe. I'm sorry."

She placed the palm of her hand on my cheek and looked into my eyes. "Thank you, Brandon. But I gotta go. What type of woman would I be if I let him fight the battle alone?"

"Dammit, Krys, it's not your fuckin' beef. That nigga has pissed off some people, especially now that he has brought you into the organization. He brought it on himself. Let him and his soldiers take care of it. I'd never forgive myself if I let you go and something happened to you. That shit would eat me up inside."

"I love you, Brandon, I do and I know that you love me more than Marcus ever could but he would never let anyone hurt me. I know Marcus and he'll protect me. Just trust me."

Carrie walked up and asked, "Are you ready to get back on the road?"

Krystal looked at me one last time and walked to the door of the truck. She got in and turned the ignition and said, "Don't worry, Brandon, I'll be okay. And who knows, maybe one day I'll never have to leave again." Then she drove out of my life.

****

CREEP

"Aye man, ain't that a detective behind you, or am I seeing things?" Trap asked while I drove down the dark highway.

I looked in my rearview mirror and cussed. "Dammit, that's Carrie's father. That muthafucka can't possibly mean us no good. I knew not to fuck with her ass again, and now we got her going to dope houses and shit. That muthafucka ain't gon' stop till he puts me away for life."

I continued to watch the car follow me but I didn't want to lead him to the trap house, although I was sure he already knew where it was. I turned down the next exit and pulled into a Taco Bell.

I looked to see if he had pulled in too. Sure enough, he pulled up behind me and blocked me in. I was thankful that me and Trap didn't have any drugs or weapons in the car which was a rarity for us because we usually stayed strapped. Detective McDonald got out of his car and walked up to my window. I rolled it down and asked, "Can I help you with something, sir? Did I do something wrong?"

"We just stepped out to get some Taco Bell, sir. Something wrong with that?" added Trap.

"Nah, ain't nothing wrong with that but I'll tell you what I do have a problem with. I don't like my daughter playing house with a fucking drug dealer." The anger in McDonald's voice was evident.

I said, "Sir, maybe you have me confused with someone else. Your daughter and I are just friends. And I don't know who told you I was a drug dealer but your information is wrong."

He gritted his teeth. "Oh yeah? Well, if I ever catch you with my daughter, I'll lock you up myself even if I have to plant drugs on you. Stay the hell away from my daughter. This is your first and last warning." He stormed back to his car and drove away.

I looked at Trap. "Carrie's ass gonna go crazy when I tell her, but that bitch got to find new friends. I'm done with that shit."

Trap laughed. "Man, that crazy bitch ain't about to leave you alone. You gon' have to kill her ass to get rid of her."

"Well, I guess her daddy better start planning a funeral."

****
MARCUS

"What's up P? Nigga are you aiight?" I asked when I answered my cell phone. It had been a minute since I talked to Paris so the phone call came as a surprise.

"Marcus, man, it's over. I got that muthafucka! I got him. Man, my girl and my baby can now rest in peace. Dawg, he's gone," Paris exclaimed through the telephone.

"Wait, man. What the fuck are you telling me P? What's happened?

He let out a small laugh. "Ditto. Ditto is gone for real, man. You should have seen his head explode. That shit felt so good. Man, me and my pops took care of his ass."

I could tell that Paris had been crying because he'd finally gotten the revenge he had been seeking. He had been looking for Ditto ever since he lost his wife and unborn son to a bomb that Ditto planted. He had also lost his mother when he was a child at Ditto's hand.

"Damn, man, that shit's really over, you got him for real dawg?"

"Yeah, Marcus, we ain't got to look over our shoulders no more. We can finally live in peace without watching our backs. I wish I could have recorded it, dawg, just so you and the crew could enjoy it," he said.

"Aiight, man, that's good. Now, you can get back out there and do your own thang. Make that money for yo' self. How do you feel about that?" I asked.

"Nah, man, I'm just gon' go ahead and step outta the game. I think it's time. I lost too many homies and people that I loved and can't replace. Me and pops gonna go somewhere and start our lives over. Maybe open up our own business and shit ya know. But I won't forget you, fam, or all that you did for me and the crew. I'll check in from time to time and if you ever need to get away, don't hesitate to call. I love you man. Take care," Paris said and hung up.

I was proud of him for the decision he'd made to leave the game alone. I had hoped that one day, I could do the same thing but I still had loose ends that needed tying up.

I had another issue on my hand now, one that would be hard for me to eliminate. My crew was getting smaller and my enemies were getting closer. I had decided that the next time I got close enough to Feelow, I would go through with it. It was a tough decision but it had to be done. I had let things get too far, and trusted that he was going to redeem himself when I let him back in. But things were worse between us than ever before. I had to find him and stop him before he stopped me, instead.

****

TYCK

"Tyck man, I need you to help me out and fix me up a hit dawg. I need a big one too so I can relax, Shit we ain't been able to chill in a minute. A nigga just wanna lay back and feel good. Know what I'm saying?"Feelow said when he laid the kilos of cocaine out on the table. We had just got back from picking up the product from Echo and I was nervous as a mutha Fucka. I hoped that I could pull it off smoothly.

I picked up the kilo that Echo had marked with an E that only I noticed. I slit the package open with a small blade and said, "Yo Fee, why won't you go ahead and get undressed while I cook this up for you real quick. Get that dick nice and ready for a nigga. Yo' ass has been hiding out on me while you have been fuckin' around with that bitch, Keisha and her bastard."

Feelow sat up straight. "Watch yo' mouth bitch. That's my muthafucka son you talking about. I don't give a fuck about the whore who's carrying him but you gonna respect my seed. Nigga you know I had to play the part until my son was born so stop trippin'. Go on and cook me some of that up. I'ma go wash off real fast and I'll be back."

As soon as he left the room, I pulled some of the ether cut cocaine out and put it in the spoon and watched it sizzle. I almost changed my mind but went ahead with the plan. As long as Feelow was in my way I could never get the chance to be Marcus' right hand. I wasn't really worried about the bitch because I could work beside her until I figured out how to get rid of her too.

I heard the shower cut off just as I poured the extra water from the spoon. I had cooked a nice enough piece and was ready for Feelow to put it in his lungs. Feelow finally walked back into the room and sat down in his favorite chair with nothing on but the beads of water from the shower he had taken. He asked, "Nigga, you got me something ready to smoke on?"

I put the piece of dope on his pipe and walked over to him. "Echo said this some new potent shit he had been dealing out. You sure you're ready for this?"

Fellow reached up and grabbed the stem from my hand. He put the flame to it to melt it and then leaned back. I pulled a chair up in front of him because I knew he liked to get freaky as soon as the smoke cleared. My heart beat faster at the anticipation of what was about to happen. Then suddenly, I felt guilty but before I could get the words out to stop him, he lit the stem and inhaled deeply.

Chapter Eleven
MARCUS

I cocked my weapon as soon as I saw Echo's ride pull up. I couldn't believe that we were still beefing over a bitch that I'd never wanted. I had been over that high school shit and was ready to move on. I stood in place and waited to see what kind of drama he would bring me.

Echo, Toe Tag, and Swag got out of the ride while I clocked every step. Toe Tag and Swag posted up by the ride, while Echo held up his hands and walked toward me. He stated, "Marcus, I come in peace. I'm here to squash this beef that we've had going on. The shit's done played. Let's call a truce."

I kept my hand on my gun because I didn't trust the nigga. He'd never given me a reason to. I looked from his crew to him and asked, "What are you here for, Echo? Because a nigga ain't believing what you talking."

"That hit on your boys was Feelow's doing. Right now that's yo' only beef. I'm here to squash your beef just like I said. That bitch from high school been off my mind. Let's call a truce and join forces. Take this whole muthafucking city to the next level," he said and then added, "I'm clean, man. Check me out. I ain't bring no fire here. A nigga just trying to live in peace. What do you say?"

I still wasn't sure. "Send yo' people away. Let it be just me and you. This is our beef, not theirs."

"Nah, nigga, whatever beef my brother has is our beef too. He is trying to push that shit to the side but you are being difficult. A nigga ain't got to me for that, so what's up?" Swag T stated.

"Swag, I got this," Echo said, and then stated to Toe Tag, "Yo' man, why don't y'all go on back. Me and Marcus got some shit to tend to." Tag started to protest but Echo held up his hand and said," I'm good, man. This nigga don't mean me no harm. I'll see y'all when I get back."

Swag and Toe Tag looked disappointed but did as their boss told them. When they drove away, Echo lifted his shirt and turned around, and then lifted his pants legs to show me that he was really unarmed. I pulled the clip from my gun and emptied the chamber so he would know that we were equal. If this was all bullshit, I would beat his ass with my bare hands.

"Get in." I nodded towards my truck. Echo nodded and walked over to the passenger side and got in. I looked around to check my surroundings and then hopped on the car, too.

As soon as I shut my door, Echo began to talk. "That beef with that bitch has been gone, my man."

"So why did you have a hit out on me when I ain't did shit?" I asked.

"Because of Carla," he said.

"Crackhead Carla. Nigga what she got to do with me? I didn't fuck with her and that shit that happened to her wasn't at my hands." I had known what Feelow did to Carla because Tyck had put me up on it. Echo had known me all my life so he should have known I would have never gone out like that on no female, not even one I didn't I give a shit about. However, I played dumb because I wasn't about to put Feelow on blast like that.

"Tag fucked with Carla like that. It was just supposed to be a trick but the nigga felt something and hoped that he could fix her," he stated.

"Man, Tag know that you can't change a bitch like that. Shit is too late for her. What the fuck was he thinking?" I replied.

"Yeah, I tried to tell him but he wasn't trying to hear that shit. Nigga just wanted to follow his heart and who was I to stop him?" Echo explained.

I pulled out of the parking lot we had been sitting in and drove slowly down the back street. I asked Echo, "So what made you realize that it wasn't me who did that foul shit?"

"Ya boy Tyck heard about the hit we had planned and stepped up. He showed Tag a video he had on his phone of Carla's torture but it wasn't you on that tape with her. It was yo' nigga, Feelow." He looked over at me to see my reaction but I wore a poker face.

124

I didn't respond to the comment right away because hearing Feelow's name tore me up. I knew then just what Echo wanted but there was no way I could deliver. I said, "So you now got that hit switched over to my boy and you think I'm gonna help you do it. What the fuck are you trying to tell me here, man? Feelow is my nigga and fucking with him ain't gonna stop a beef, it's gonna make it bigger. Regardless of the shit that nigga had done, dawg. I can't go against him like that."

Echo replied, "Man, Fellow did some foul ass hits and his ass needs to be taught a lesson. I'm here outta respect to let you know that when I get in that, it doesn't have shit to do with you."

"So you saying when you strike that I'm just supposed to sit back and watch you?" My forehead was wrinkled.

"Nah, fam, all I'm saying is to stay outta the way. You a good nigga, Marcus. Fee done did some unforgivable shit, not only to us, but to you. He gon have to answer for that."

"Man, that's my brother but you're right. Fee made his own choices and I can't do shit to change that. Muthafucka is getting worse as the days pass," I said and then went silent for a minute before I stated, "Aiight man, we good and I'm gon' stay back so you can handle what you need to handle, with no retaliation. I give you my word."

Echo smiled. "Facts, and on the strength of you, I'ma try to make it swift and painless."

****

TYCK

"Tyck. Nigga, something doesn't feel right. What the fuck did I just smoke? Bitch, did you put something in my shit? My head is fucking pounding. What the fuck's going on? Nigga, something's wrong," Feelow cried out after he exhaled the smoke he had held in his lungs for a couple of minutes.

I watched as his arms jerked as if he was going into a seizure. I was amazed at how quickly the drug caused his body to spasm .He tried to reach out for me but I moved back. I pulled another chair in front of him but left some distance between us. I wanted to watch the show as his ass reaped what he held sowed. I taunted him. "How do you feel, bitch? Shit doesn't feel so good when someone else has the upper hand, does it?" I laughed and continued to watch the show.

"What the fuck did you give me? What was in that shit, muthafucka? Huh? I'm, I'm gonna kill yo' ass when I get my hands on you," Feelow cried out but I felt no sympathy for him.

Feelow was a piece of shit and it was time someone showed him. Marcus had forgiven him for so much and yet, he still shit on him. I asked, "What are you gonna do now, Fee? Huh nigga? You had to do that shit to that girl. She didn't do nothing to nobody. And Marcus, nigga that's yo' brother and he ain't never did you dirty but you fucked him over every chance you got. You deserve this shit and I'm glad that I could assist Echo and his crew in completing the task."

"Fuck! Fuck! Fuck you, Tyck! Nigga, it's gonna take more than a hit of that shit to get rid of me," Feelow wailed.

"That's that ether cut, nigga. That's gonna slowly make you lose your mind until you kill yo' own self. Dick ain't so hard now, is it, bitch?"

Feelow looked down between his legs at his limp dick and laughed. "Nigga, you had some lame ass head anyway. I'm coming for you, Tyck. I give you my word on that."

"Yeah, with what little bit of mind you're gonna have left. Now maybe Marcus will see my worth. I've been waiting for this day to come. I deserve a spot next to him, and unlike you, I ain't gonna let a bitch discourage me. You were disloyal to him so he will never trust you again." I stood up from the chair when I noticed he was temporarily paralyzed from the drug, a side effect that seemed very unpleasant. I put another hit on the pipe and melted it and then put it to Feelow's mouth and said, "Inhale bitch. Suck on this muthafucking glass like it's a real dick."

Feelow tried to turn his head but couldn't and I knew he would only be able to hold his breath for so long. As soon as I saw he needed to inhale some air, I put the lighter to the end of the glass and struck it. I could have sworn that I saw a tear forming in the corner of his left eye, so I said, "Uh oh. A nigga like you cries? Hell, I never even knew you had a heart." I laughed and put that stem down and then went into the kitchen to gather the rest of the cocaine.

I left the one brick that I had used to drug him just for special effects. I wiped down everything I had touched just to be safe and headed for the door. Before I walked out, I went back over to him and bent down to whisper in his ear. "I'll take real good care of him." Then, I walked out and slammed the door behind me and never once looked back.

****

MARCUS

I asked Micro to bring his sister and meet me at the warehouse. I had to find out what she knew. I had hoped that maybe she heard names being said. I was certain that if she had been present when Blow took the bullet, he had gotten Trigger to speak. I paced the wooden floor and tried to make sense of all the shit that had happened.

Me and Echo finally making a truce had come at the right time. However, I didn't want him to touch Feelow. That would be my job. After all we said and done, I couldn't even understand how I still had love in my heart for him. I looked at the time and noticed that micro was running late so I picked up my phone to call just to make sure shit was right on his end. Before I was able to punch in all the numbers, I heard the vehicle pull in.

I opened the door to find Detective McDonald instead. He asked me as soon as he saw me, "Marcus, how did you know I was coming to visit?"

"Is there something I can help you with, detective?" I asked in a polite yet serious tone.

"Well, word on the street is that my daughter has been hanging out with your girlfriend, but I don't listen to hearsay. I decided it would be best if I came and heard it from the horse's mouth. So, where is she, Marcus?"

"I don't know who you're talking about so I can't help you. Besides, I don't answer to you," I said.

"So, Mr. Newsome, you're telling me that you don't have a girlfriend by the name of Krystal Madison. I could have sworn I've seen you two together before," he replied as he looked around trying to find evidence.

"I decided to tell him the truth hoping to make him go away, I didn't want micro to pull up while he was there and cause Tina to get spooked. I replied, "Yeah, my bitch is named Krystal but she doesn't do shit so what's the issue with your daughter and her being friends. Scared your little princess is gonna slip on some black dick. Might do her some good."

His nose flared as if my comment had made him angry but I didn't really give a fuck. His anger was what I was aiming for. I was clean at that moment so he could kiss my black ass.

He nodded his head and said, "Just a little warning to you and your crew. If I find out that you have my daughter doing illegal activities, it won't be bail you'll need. It would be a funeral director instead."

I laughed but took heed to what he'd said and made up my mind to tell Krystal that she would have to find another bitch to make those runs because the thing I cherished more than my life was my money and I'd be damned if I let a bitch stop me from getting it.

I pulled my phone back out but before I had a chance to dial, Micro and his sister pulled up. They got out of the car and we all walked inside. Micro asked, "Yo' man, was that a cop that I just passed pulling out of here?"

"Yeah. Muthafucka is looking for his daughter but his threats don't faze a nigga like me. I got more important shit to deal with." I looked down at Tina who stood around five feet tall. I could see the pain in her eyes from the heartbreak of losing Blow. I wondered if Micro knew that she and Blow had been fucking before he died. I asked, "What's up, Tina? You good, lil mama?"

She nodded her head. "Yeah, I'm gonna be okay. I just can't believe he's gone. I feel like I'm in a nightmare and can't wake up."

I looked at Micro for his reaction and when he noticed, he said, "It's all good, dawg. I've known for a minute now but never said anything because I knew Blow was a good nigga. Shits straight. Just wish we could have saved him, man."

"Yeah, he was a good nigga. One of the best on my team. But now we gotta clap back. We can't let this shit go unpunished. That's where you come in, Tina. I need you to tell me anything that you may have heard. Just go slow. Come on over here and sit down and start from the beginning,." I pulled a chair up for her to hopefully make her more comfortable. I never had a beef with Trigger so I just needed the name of who sent him.

With saddened eyes, she looked at Micro and then back at me and then she told me everything. "Me and Blow were chilling in the room with the music and shit playing. Black was in the living room keeping post and handling business. Well, things became intense between me and Blow and I may have been a little loud so he turned the music up. We never heard anyone at the door." She took a deep breath and then continued. "Blow stopped right when I was about to... Well, you know, I asked him what was wrong and he said he'd heard something. He got his gun out of the drawer and told me not to leave the room unless I heard a gunshot." Her tears began to form and Micro held her hand so she could finish. "When I heard the shot, I froze at first. I heard Blow asking the man who had sent him. Blow called him Trigger. It sounded like he knew him. I wanted to run out and help him but I was so scared. I've never learned how to shoot a gun and I just wanted to save Blow. Oh my God, I can't believe he's really gone."

Her tears broke me down a notch but I had to keep her talking. "Tina, you said that Blow asked Trigger who had sent him. Did he give him a name? You gotta tell me whose name he said. Who sent Trigger to my crew?"

She looked me in my eyes and replied, "he said Feelow sent him."

Corey Robinson

****
ECHO

"I pulled it off. That bastard took a hit and damn near lost his mind. That shit was funny as a muthafucka," Tyck laughed, and told me about how it all went down. "Then before I left, and while he couldn't move, I piled the pipe up again and put it to his lips. I wanted to stay and watch but I didn't want to get hemmed up if it got outta hand. Man, that shit was Oscar-worthy."

I looked at Toe Tag and Swag T and nodded my head at them. They both got up and left the room because they understood what I was telling them. When they were gone, I said to Tyck. "You did good. That nigga did a lot of bad shit to other people and deserved it. Nigga, you seem mighty happy about it. What's up with that? I thought you and that nigga were bumping dicks and shit. What happened?"

"Man, I ain't gon lie, I was feeling Feelow at first but that nigga ain't loyal to nobody so, I knew eventually he would stab me in the back the same way he did Marcus. I still don't understand why he and Marcus fell out, however, now I can get the spot I deserve," he said with excitement.

I already knew what he meant but I asked anyway, "What do you mean you can now get the spot you deserve? The fuck are you talking about, T?"

Tyck replied, "The spot beside Marcus. I ain't worried about the white bitch. I 'll eventually push her out but until then, I'm gon' ride and prove my worth."

About that time, Tag and Swag T came back into the room with rolls of duct tape and a chair. Swag T also carried a sledge-hammer. Tyck noticed what they had in their hands and asked, "Man, why do they have all that shit?"

I smiled at Tyck. "My nigga, that shit is for you."

"But why? I did what you asked and eliminated the problem. So, what's going on, Echo?" he asked in a shaky voice.

I sat forward and placed my elbow on my knees and then put my hands together as if I were going to pray. Once I looked up at Tag and winked, he knew what it meant and pulled his Glock out and pointed it at Tyck's head. Tyck asked again, "Echo man, what the fuck is going on? I'm on yo' side in this. Don't do this, man."

I nodded my head and said, "Sit yo' punk ass down."

Swag T put her hands on his shoulders and pushed him down in his seat. He tried to resist but was met with the butt of the gun. Toe Tag then passed his gun to me and I kept it on Tyck while Tag taped his ankles to the legs of the chair. He then taped his arms to the armrests. Tyck started to plead for his life but Tag stopped him by putting a strip of tape over his mouth. Only his eyes could be seen from under the tape. "Ya know, Tyck, at one time you were fuckin' with Feelow real heavy, and yet, it was so easy for you to betray him."

Bam! "MMM.MMM.MM.HM,HM." Tyck began sweating and his face turned a bright red but I still had some more to say to him. "Now, the way I see it is, you are trying to get up under Marcus and you'll do anything to get there." Bam! "Oh I'm sorry, was that your hand, I heard crack?"

I stood in front of him and looked him in his sneaky eyes and said, "See, I give you an order to do something to Feelow to test you and I'm glad that I did because you showed me that you are a disloyal muthafucka. You see, Feelow didn't mean shit to me so, I owe him nothing. But you, mmm, mmm, mmm, you were his bitch. You've sucked and fucked that nigga to sleep at night. You've made runs with him and he even trusted you enough to put you up on his plans to eliminate a nigga who treated him as his own brother. So, you owed Feelow that loyalty and respect."

Bam!

"You see how painful it is to be hit by this sledgehammer? Huh muthafucka? Well, that's how it feels to be betrayed by a bitch you trusted. That shit hurts. Now you wanna sit on the throne beside Marcus, but lil nigga, that shit ain't gon' happen. The last thing he needs in his crew is another disloyal bastard."

Tyck squeezed his eyes closed. When he opened them, tears fell down his cheeks. I couldn't feel any remorse for him because of his betrayal. If he betrayed a nigga he was fucking, he would betray anyone. I would be less than a man if I let his ass live another day. Marcus and I had just called a truce and letting Tyck worm his way up under him would cause us another setback so, I did what was best.

"You are a snake, Tyck, and I don't fuck with snakes too heavy. I was kinda hoping that you wouldn't go against Feelow but you let a nigga down. I won't let you do the same thing to Marcus. May God have mercy on your soul. Bitch."

And then, I swung with all my might and busted his skull wide open.

****

MARCUS

"Aye, that bitch gotta go. She ain't running with this crew. Get rid of her ass," I said to Krystal with a serious look on my face.

"Marcus, who else am I gonna get to do it. I don't know any females. Shit, you know more bitches than me; get one of them dumb ass hoes that let you slide," Krystal said with her hands on her hips and a voice full of attitude.

"Yeah, so, I get to hear yo ass bitch every night cause you gon swear a nigga getting his dick wet. Hell no, you just gonna have to keep doing the runs," I said and pulled her onto the bed. "Besides, I think that nigga likes you."

"Fuck you, Marcus. I'm sending Carrie on the next run by herself," said Krystal.

"Nah, lil mama, that bitch's muthafuckin daddy gonna have my black ass in jail for that shit so, you might as well prepare yourself for the next run too," I said right when my phone rang. Krystal started to speak but I held a hand up to stop her and answered my phone, "Yo what up Kita? You aiight?" Krystal looked at me sideways when I said Kita's name but I wasn't studying her ass.

Kita cried into the phone, "Marcus, the police just left here. Oh my God, I can't believe it. Marcus they found Tyckori in a ditch with his brains leaking out of his skull. His hands and knees were crushed too. What am I gonna do?"

I put my head down to mourn the soldier. "Kita, do you know anything about who could have done this?" I asked, but I already knew the answer to my own question before she answered me.

"I don't know, Marcus. The last person he was with was Feelow, but I hate to think that Feelow would do something like that to him. They had gotten really close. So it had to be someone else."

I thought about Echo telling me that Tyck showed him the video of Feelow torturing Carla and wondered if Feelow had found out somehow. But then again, I wanted it to be someone else. Maybe he had sent Trigger back to take care of Tyck like Blow and Black. I told myself that I needed to see Feelow and fix the problem. I said to Kita, "Don't worry, I'm gonna find out who did that. In the meantime I'ma handle the funeral costs for Tyck, okay?"

She sniffed back tears. "Thank you, Marcus. Please find out who did that." She hung up.

My set was getting smaller and smaller and I knew that it was time I handled the situation. I looked at Krystal and said, "Your ass ain't going back out in the streets until this situation with Feelow is over." She started to protest but I stood up and said, "My crew is getting dropped one by one and until I get who is responsible for it, nobody affiliated with me is safe." My phone rang again and when I saw that it was Echo, I answered, "Sup, dawg."

"Marcus, I ran into a snake in the hood and took care of it. It was about to slither your way and I couldn't let that happen."

I listened as he spoke and instantly thought that he was talking about Feelow. I interrupted him, "Nigga, I told you that was my job so why you---"

"Nah, man, not that one. You had another one slithering. I got your back, though, so don't worry I'm gonna always be a step ahead so that your path will be clear. You can thank me later."

I was about to say something else but realized he had already hung up. I felt in my gut that he was talking about Tyck. I didn't know about Echo but he had never committed a senseless murder. When he offends a bitch, you could be rest assured that they deserved it. I started to get dressed and told Krystal, "Call Carrie and tell her to chill for a minute. I got to handle this okay and then we'll talk about those Baltimore trips."

"I'm going with you, Marcus." She began to put on some sweats and a T-shirt. Even dressed down, her ass was beautiful.

I shook my head. "The hell you are! I can't let you come with me on this run so please, just lay yo ass down. I'll be back."

"Hell no, you want me to lay my ass down and wonder if you're going to make it back to me. Not this time. You trained me for times like this, so it's time to use what I learned."

I smiled because I knew that I had created a boss bitch and when she fully blossomed, she would be a force to be reckoned with. "Aiight. Get yo' piece because we are going on a manhunt and we ain't coming back till we find him."

****
FEELOW

What the fuck happened? I feel like shit, I said to myself when I woke up from a long nap; one I didn't think I had taken intentionally. When I got up off the floor, I almost fell over the coffee table. I tried to remember what had happened and it vaguely came back to me.

I walked into my kitchen and saw the brick of cocaine still on the table. I remembered Tyck filling my pipe with the cooked-up powder and then how my body and mind reacted.

That's that Ether cut, nigga, I could still hear Tyck's voice say as he laughed in my face. But I couldn't understand why he had done that to me. *Marcus had to have made him do it.* stood and stared at the product. *He must have somehow convinced Tyck to slide the brick of Ether cut in with the rest.* I couldn't believe that Tyck had done that shit to me but who was I to judge because I had done that same thing to Marcus. I stabbed him in the back with his own blade and had been steady jiggin' it in ever since.

"That muthafucka is going to pay for that shit. I'm gon' hit Marcus black ass where it really hurts. Bitch ass ain't even gonna see it coming," I said out loud and went to gather a few things I needed for the task that I had ahead of me.

I was about to get the ultimate payback and couldn't wait to see the look on Marcus' face when he arrived at the destination I was going to be at. After I had everything I would need, I grabbed my keys and got in my truck. Vengeance was mine and was only a few miles away.

Corey Robinson

Chapter Twelve
KEISHA

The pain was intense and worse than any I had ever felt before. "Ugh. Oh my God," I cried out as I held my stomach and slid down with my back against the wall, to the floor. Not even two minutes later, another sharp pain hit me. I tried to stand back up so I could get to my phone and call an ambulance and suddenly felt something wet between my legs. I knew then that I didn't have much longer. Khalif was ready to see the world and I didn't have a choice but to let him.

Since it was hard for me to stand, I crawled on all fours to get to the table where my phone laid. I dialed 911 and another contraction hit me like a ton of bricks. "Ahhh!"

I heard the operator on the line ask., "Hello, is anyone there? This is 911 emergency. How can I help you? Are you alright?"

"I-I'm-Aaah, I think my baby is ready to come out. Help me. Aaah." I could tell that Khalif was going to have the same fierce attitude as his father, but when I thought about it, it made me miss Feelow. I wanted him to be there when our son entered the world but I was scared as hell to call him.

"Ma'am, where is your location? Are you by yourself?" she asked.

Her questions came quick and made me dizzy. I had started to fade in and out of consciousness but managed to hold on long enough to tell her where I was and what was going on. "I'm at 447 Lake Street and I'm in labor. Please. It hurts. Please help, and then, I passed out.

* * * *

CARRIE

"How dare you, Daddy. You had no fucking right to go to my friends and threaten them. What the hell were you thinking?"I asked with an attitude. I was mad as hell and wanted to make him see that I wasn't a little girl anymore. It was time he stopped running my life.

"You're my daughter, Carrie and I won't stand by and allow you to fall in with a company like that. I mean, look how you're talking to me. You've never disrespected me like that before and now that you're hanging out with a bunch of hoodlums, you talk to me like I'm a pile of shit," he replied in a loud voice. I could see the look of disappointment on his face and felt kinda bad but he had to let me grow up and learn on my own.

"Daddy, I know that you're afraid that something is going to happen to me but I'm in good hands. Besides, you know my ass is crazy and can roll with the best of them. Those people don't mean me any harm. Please just try and understand.' I stared and smiled hoping that it would touch his heart.

He let out a loud sigh and said, "I can't turn a blind eye to their illegal activities, Carrie. That would make me just as bad as them if I did. So, if you wanna be grown and deal in the things they deal in, so be it, but don't think for one second that I'm going to save you if your ass gets locked up." He stood up from the seat he had sat in and shook his head. "If that's how you wanna live your life, then I suggest you live it somewhere else. I want you outta my house by the time I get in from work," and then, he walked out.

I was so shocked I couldn't speak. I knew he was mad but I never thought he would kick me out of the house that he had raised me in. It was times like these that I missed my mother the most. She never would have let him put me out and she would have stood by me no matter what decision I made. I walked upstairs to my room so I could pack my belongings and try to figure out where I was going. I couldn't stay with Creep because even though he denied it,

I knew that other bitches were still creeping around. I would have to beat a bitch's ass everyday to get my point across.

I thought about Hey Man and Karma and knew that I couldn't leave them behind. They were my life. I damn sure wasn't going to ask Krystal to put me up. There's no way we could have lived under the same roof besides, her man was a whore and I didn't want to entertain his drama. I reached in my purse and found the number I had been given when I rode with Krystal to Baltimore. I opened the small folded piece of paper and picked up my phone. When the person on the other end answered, I froze at first but then, I got to the point.

"I need a place to stay. Can you help me out? My daddy just kicked me out, "I said and waited patiently for the answer.

When he told me what I wanted to hear, I smiled and hung up. I knew that Krystal was going to be pissed but at that moment, I didn't care. I'd cross that road when I got to it.

A bitch needed a place to rest her head and I didn't care whose toes I stepped on to get it.

****
FEELOW

"Sup, Tammy. You wanna chill with me tonight?"I asked when I pulled up beside her. I had hoped that she was no longer mad about the situation with Keisha. They were family and blood was thicker than water so, Keisha would forgive her before she would forgive me.

"Fuck you, Feelow. Your ass is just trying to con me into telling you where my cousin is but the bitch ain't gonna tell me shit no more because of you," she said with a slight attitude but I wasn't going to give up.

"Damn girl, cut a nigga a break. Come on."

When I saw a smile pop up on her face, I knew that she was done. She put her hand on her hips and asked, "Why you ain't tell me that she's pregnant with yo' baby? It's foul as fuck for you to fuck me after you done housed up with my cousin and a made family. You ain't shit, Feelow."

She looked at me funny and caused me to ask, "The fuck you looking like that for. Hell is your damn problem?"

She shrugged her shoulders and asked, "Why do you keep twitching? I ain't never seen you do that before. Your ass ain't on drugs, are you?"

Besides Tyck, Marcus, and Keisha, no one else knew what I did, at least to my knowledge. I wanted to keep it that way for as long as I could. "Girl, the only drug I'm trying to be on is you. Come on, a nigga needs some medication."

She smacked her lips. "I don't know why I'm gonna do that because you really ain't shit, Feelow, but you do have some good dick and a bitch like me appreciates that. But if you mention Keisha's name one time, I'm out."

"Damn girl, aiight. Now, get yo fine ass in," I said and watched her walk around the front of the car to the passenger side. I pushed the door open for her and when she got in, I immediately said, "Now, go on and take them panties off for a nigga, and play wit that pussy."

That shit I had been set up to smoke had fucked up my sex drive. I had to see if my dick could still get hard so I needed Tammy to do something freaky for me. She looked at me like I was crazy but her ass was gonna do what I said one way or the other.

She asked, "Why do you want me to do it while we are in the car? Can't you wait till we get to your place or wherever we are going?"

I shook my head and patted her thigh. "Nah, a nigga is trying to see that fat muthafuka now so do that shit or I can go find me a bitch that will." As soon as I said that, she undid her shorts and pulled them and her panties off. She cocked her legs up in the seat and did as I told her. I licked my lips and then unzipped my pants so I could pull my lil man out. My shit was limp as a noddle. "Stick a finger up there and then put that shit in my mouth so I can get a little taste."

Once again, Tammy did as I said. I felt myself being turned on but no matter how much I jacked my dick, it would not stiffen. I was getting angrier by the second. Tammy made it even worse when she asked, "Nigga, what the fuck is wrong with you?

Actually, what's wrong with me? Why your dick ain't getting hard, Feelow. That shits crazy as fuck."

I put my dick back in my pants with a disappointed look on my face, saying, "I guess I better wait like you said. Feels kinda crazy doing that shit with all these cars passing by. Put yo' clothes back on. I have to tap that ass later because I got one stop to make before we chill."Tammy put her clothes back on and let out a heavy sigh. I couldn't believe the shit that had just happened and it made me even more determined than ever to get at Marcus, and I knew just what to do to allure him to me.

****

KEISHA

When I opened my eyes, I was groggy and a little confused at first but then, my baby kicked me. I quickly remember what had happened. "Oh my god, I gotta get out of here," I said. I hated hospitals and my calling for an ambulance to take me to one didn't make it any better.

I started to pull the monitor off my arm right when a nurse walked in. "Uh uh Miss Watson, I wouldn't do that if I were you."

I looked up at her like she was crazy and started to speak but another contraction knocked the words right out of my mouth, "Ahh shit. shit .shit. Damn, is this supposed to hurt like that?" I asked.

The nurse smiled. "Don't worry, when it's all over and you're holding that little life in your hands, you'll forget all that you went through.' She put the stethoscope over my belly to listen and then asked, "Is there someone you want us to call to be here for you? That little one isn't staying in there much longer."

I thought about Feelow and wished that I could call him but wasn't sure if it was a good idea. He deserved to see his firstborn come into the world but my fear outweighed my kindness. I remembered Marcus had told me that when I had my son, Feelow was going to eliminate me, I didn't know if Marcus was lying or not but I was too afraid to take that chance. I couldn't call Marcus either because if Feelow found out I'd called him to be there instead, all hell would really break loose. I didn't have anyone else but deep inside my heart, I knew I didn't want to be alone, so, I called the only family I had left.

Tammy had already sold me out to Feelow once, but I'd hoped I could depend on her not to do it again. She had always had a thing for Feelow and me ending up with him wasn't something I'd planned. I was trying to get Marcus to wife me up but because I had fucked so many other niggas, he dismissed my ass. I seriously thought that getting with his boy would make him rethink it but of course, it backfired and my dumb ass got pregnant.

I dialed Tammy's cell phone number and when she picked, up I said, "Tammy, I need you."

It took her a second to respond but she finally said, "Fuck you, Keisha. You knew I had a thing for Feelow but you still fucked him and on top of that, your ass got pregnant. Bitch, I should be the one carrying his baby, not you."

I rolled my eyes and as soon as I did, I felt another contraction, "Aaah, Aash, shit. Shit. Please Tammy, I don't have anyone else. Please I'm at the hospital about to have my baby and I just want someone familiar here with me, please."

"What's the matter? Marcus ain't gonna rescue you again or better yet. Why your ass ain't calling Feelow, ain't he the muthafuckin' daddy?" she replied.

"Look, I'm asking for you to be here Tammy. You and nobody else. You're the only family I got left and it would mean so much to me if you came. Please, aaah,uh,uh, uh! Please, Tammy, he'll be coming out soon. Are you coming or not?" I cried.

"I'm a little busy right now with my man but if I get done in time, I'll be there." Coldly, she hung up.

I wondered if the man she was talking about was Feelow. Somehow, my gut instinct said that I was right. I picked the phone back up to make another call but before I could dial, Khalif sent me another shot of pain, "Ahh, nurse get this muthafucka out of me, get him the fuck out!"

A slew of nurses ran into the room and the doctor got between my legs to examine me. When he was done, he told one of the nurses to fit me on a mask. She left my side immediately and when she returned, she covered my face with a clear mask. My eyes instantly became heavy and before I could get the nurse's attention to remove the mask, my eyes closed.

****

I couldn't believe that bitch had the nerve to call me and ask me to go to the hospital to hold her hand while she brought that bastard into the world. When Feelow returned to the car, he asked me, "Who were you on the phone with?"

I was not about to tell him that I had just talked to Keisha or that she was about to have his baby. I knew he would have dissed me once again for her if he knew. So instead, I did the only thing I could and lied. "Oh, that was a dumb ass nigga I used to fuck with thinking he could convince me to take him back," I said.

Feelow looked at me sideways and stated, "Oh yes. So you ain't gon' give the nigga another chance. I mean you can do what you want as long as that pussy stays wet for me when I want it. Know what I'm saying.

His comment made me blush and gave me an attitude at the same time. I needed Feelow to want me for himself and now that muthafucka basically said that he would share me. I smiled a fake smile and said, "So do you mind another man fucking me as long as you can still hit it? You ain't shit Feelow. I don't even know why I fall for your bullshit."I crossed my arms over my chest and looked out the window. I felt Fellow's hand under my chin and then, he pulled to turn my head back to him. He said, "Ah girl, you know I'm just fucking with you. That's my pussy now and if I find out another nigga runs up in it, I'm cutting that shit up. That shit's too good to share."

I pulled my head away and turned to look back out the window. It had started to lightly drizzle, and I watched as the pellets of water came down. I was about to give in and tell Feelow that

Keisha was giving birth to his baby right then but when he pulled into the driveway in front of a small brick home, I thought better of it. I grabbed the door handle to get out when he did but he stopped me, explaining, "Nah, this is my ol' girl's house and she will have my ass if I let you up in here, so, just chill out here. I'ma leave the keys in the ignition so you can listen to some jams but don't drive off in my shit or I'm gonna come looking for you and when I find you, I promise you'll regret it."

I shut my door back lightly and leaned the seat back. Somehow, I felt like I was in for a long night. I heard Feelow knock on the door and I lifted my head up just in time to see an attractive older woman open the door. They talked for a second and then, an older man came up behind the woman. I smiled to myself and hoped that one day, I could meet his mother. I started to lay my head back down but saw Feelow pull out his gun and shoot the man in the head. "Oh my God, "I said out loud and then covered my mouth with my hands. I didn't know what else that was going to happen and wasn't about to watch and find out so, I leaned my head back, shut my eyes, said a prayer, and hoped that God would hear me.

****

FEELOW

"Oh my God, why did you shoot him? He didn't do anything to you. What is wrong with you, Keyshawn? Oh my God, please help him," Gloria cried out but her cries didn't mean shit to me, and neither did her husband who was lying on the floor dying from a bullet wound. I pointed the gun down at her and said, "Get the fuck up"

"No, Keyshawn. He's gonna die if we don't help him. I won't tell anybody it was you, I promise but please don't let him die!"she pleaded. I moved the gun from her head and turned it on her husband and pulled the trigger a second time. When his head opened up, she screamed "Nooo, no no no no."

"Now, get yo' ass up like I told you to do," I exclaimed. "Muthafucka could have still been breathing if your ass would have just listened the first time."

I yanked her up by the arm and pushed her ahead of me. When I got to the kitchen, I made her sit in a chair and be quiet. I pulled out the black electrical tape that I had stashed in my pocket earlier and when I did, she started to cry. "Keyshawn no. Son, why are you doing this? What have I ever done to you to deserve this?"

I pushed the tip of the gun to the middle of her forehead and said, "I'm not your muthafucking son. Your son is why I'm here now so you can thank him for this."

"Marcus? No Marcus, don't even talk to me. He hasn't in years. He's hated me ever since I let James convince me to kick him out. So, whatever you're trying to get from him is not going to work out. He doesn't give a damn about me."Gloria stated why she breathed heavily. But I knew she was lying. Marcus was kicked out by her because she had chosen the love of a man over him, but he had forgiven her almost a year ago. He never told anyone the truth because he never wanted someone using her as bait like I was doing.

I sat my gun on the table and taped up her legs and arms but left her mouth free. I was going to use her to lure Marcus to me and then, I would kill both of them together. When I had her taped up, I said, "I'm going to need you to talk to Marcus and convince him to come over here. It shouldn't be too hard because I know y'all made up long ago, so, you can stop the lies and bullshit about him hating you."

She shook her head, and with tears in her eyes, said, "I will not lure my son here so you can kill him. I'll die first, so go ahead and do what you need to."

I hit her with the butt of the gun and said, "Bitch, you'll do what the fuck I say. That lil nigga gonna eat one of these pieces of lead whether you call him or not. At least this way, y'all can say your goodbyes."

"Keyshawn, what happened to y'all? You were best friends growing up. Not even the air could separate y'all. Whatever's going on y'all need to work it out. Yall are like brothers. Don't let anything come between that," she stated but her words didn't phase me.

I pulled my phone out of my pocket and dialed Marcus' number. It rang a few times before he finally answered, "Is there a reason why you're calling me, Feelow?"

I pushed the phone in Ms. Gloria's face and she turned her head and said, "No, I can't do it."

I could hear Marcus from the other side. "Nigga, is that my momma? Where the fuck are you, Feelow? Nigga, you better not harm her or I will kill your ass for real. I've spared you long enough."

I laughed and put my phone to my ear. "Yeah, Marcus that would be mommy dearest. I just thought I'd to stop by and pay her a visit for old time's sake. You know, catch up on some things."

"You're at her house? How the fuck did you know where she lived?

"Oh Marcus, I know more than you think. Why don't just stop by for a second. I'm sure she would enjoy your company," I taunted, and then I hung up. I knew he was gonna show up so, I prepared myself for the visit.

****

MARCUS

I immediately jumped up and went to the frame on the wall and put my hand on it so that I could access the secret room. When I got downstairs, I pulled open the cabinet that I held my weapons.

Krystal came down the stairs. "Marcus, what are you doing? What's wrong?" she asked.

"I'm about to kill that muthafucka. I can't let it slide anymore."

"Who Marcus? Who are you talking about? Stop and answer me."

I stopped and with a murderous look, I replied, "Feelow! That muthafucka got my momma held at gunpoint. I should have been killed his ass. Fuck!"

"Your mother? Marcus, I thought you hated your mother. I didn't even know y'all still communicated." Krystal's curious look was accentuated by a raised brow.

"Does it matter? I'm a man and I'd be dead wrong if I don't save her. Now, you can either stand there and look at me crazy or you can come pick out a gun and have my back. Your choice," I said as I loaded the chamber and clip.

She shrugged her shoulders in submission. "You think I'm gonna let you go on a murder mission alone? Hell no." She went to the cabinet and picked out a nine millimeter.

We suited up with bulletproof vests and pocketed extra ammo. When we got in the jeep, I turned to her and said, "Thanks for always having my back." We headed off to trap a snake that I should have killed long ago.

****

TAMMY

"What in the hell is taking him so damn long?"I asked out loud as if someone was going to answer me. Feelow had been in that house for almost an hour and didn't seem to be coming out anytime soon. I finally turned the radio off because it was irritating the fuck outta me. I thought about Keisha and felt bad for not being there for her. She was family and there I was letting a piece of dick come between us. I vowed that after Feelow got done doing whatever the fuck he was doing, I was going to have him drop me off a couple of blocks from the hospital so I could go see my cousin.

I looked at the clock on the dashboard one more time and said to myself, "This muthafucka needs to come out or I'm gonna go in there and get him." I started to bite my nails, a habit I had every time I got nervous. I thought about the man I saw Feelow shoot and wondered what kind of beef they'd had to make him do that.

Fuck it. I'm coming in to get you. As soon as I opened the car door, I saw a set of car lights coming down the gravel driveway. I hurriedly shut the door back and ducked down so I couldn't be seen.

I listened to the car cut off and the door being slammed. I then heard footsteps come closer to the car I had just ducked down in. I was scared as hell because I didn't know who was out there. I just prayed really hard and hoped that they didn't see me.

The footsteps finally became distant so I slowly crept up and peeked out of the front window. I saw two people going toward the house and upon closer inspection, I noticed that it was Marcus and some white girl. *Hmph, must be that bitch he was fucking with.*

I could tell that the visit was one that wasn't welcomed from the way they had crept up. I wanted to warn Feelow but I was too damn scared to move. I watched as Marcus opened the front door and ran in. When he bent down and put his hand on the man's neck, he shook his head and I knew that meant the man had no pulse.

Marcus closed the door behind himself and left the girl outside. I would make sure to keep my eyes on her because I'd be damned if they double-teamed Feelow. If it hadn't been for Feelow, I would have dialed 911 but I couldn't bear the thought of them putting him in handcuffs. So instead, I decided to keep watch just in case I needed to beat somebody's ass.

****

MARCUS

"Well, well, well. Look who decided to join us. Welcome to the party, Marcus. We were just discussing which one of her fingers I should chop off first. Which one do you think I should do?" Feelow had an evil smile on his face. I looked at my mother and my heart broke. Her eyes were already swollen shut and I could tell that she was in serious pain.

I couldn't believe that a brotherhood once so strong had come to this. "Why man? Why are you doing this? I thought we had bonded this shit back up. What the fuck man?" I asked Feelow.

"Yeah, Marcus, we did something but it wasn't a bond. Nigga, you caused this scene here. Ever since you met that white bitch, it's like you lost your damn mind. Your dumb ass had the nerve to give that bitch my spot. I've been with you from day one, Marcus. Nigga, you've had my loyalty since we were kids. I never turned you away on those nights you needed a place to lay your head. Never! But nigga, you get pussy-whipped and forget who the fuck had yo' back all these years."

"Feelow, man, my momma ain't got shit to do with what we got going on. Dawg, this shit is between *us*. You pushed us apart when you told your first lie. Nigga, yo' ass been tripping ever since Ditto tried you. But real talk, Fee, I didn't have shit to do with it. You are my best friend man, my nigga. My muthafucking bro. You got Trigger killing off my crew and trying to rob me because of what? Because your crackhead ass didn't believe in anything about the damn pipe. I forgave yo ass for everything and, yet, you still want more." Tears formed in my eyes.

He laughed and leaned forward in the chair he sat in and said, "More? You said I want more? Nah, nigga, I only wanted what was rightfully mine but you gave that to a white bitch. What the fuck does that bitch know about you and these streets? Huh? But I know. My nigga, I feel everything you feel but that shit doesn't matter to you as long as you are getting what you want. You got me showing that bitch around crack houses and shit and her dumb ass talking about helping. The fuck is wrong wit' yo' ass, nigga? Pussy has made you soft. So, fuck you."

"Nah, bro, you got it all wrong," I said.

He stood up and pointed the gun at my mother's chest and asked, "Why you never told me that you and your mama had made amends? Huh Marcus? What else didn't you tell me? You gave Tyck that kilo of Ether cut and convinced him to make me smoke it, huh? Well, he did but it only fucked with my mind for a minute. A real nigga like me don't fall that easy."

I looked at him, confused. "What the fuck are you talking about, man? I don't know shit about no Ether cut."

"Who else would have done that shit? That nigga was talking about blasting yo' bitch and taking her spot and you trusted him to get rid of me," Fellow stated.

"Nah, man, I'm telling you that wasn't me that did that. Where the fuck I'm gonna get some Ether cut? Come on, Fee, just put the gun down and let's talk about this like men."

About that time, I saw Krystal creep in the back door and come up behind him. As soon as Feelow cocked his gun, I saw the iron pipe she had in her hand. She quickly cracked him over the head and knocked him the fuck out.

"Shit. Damn baby, you're right on time. Find a knife and cut that tape off my mother, then help me drag his ass to the truck. I'm gonna take his ass somewhere and beat the shit outta him." Krystal agreed and found a knife in one of the kitchen drawers and cut my mother free. My mother began to cry. I told her," Go upstairs until I pull out of here. When I leave, wait ten minutes and call the police. Tell them someone broke in and shot your husband and then attacked you. Tell them you don't know who it was but you think it was an old street beef your husband had. You understand? I'll be back to check on you later."

My mother looked from me to Krystal but then turned and ran up the stairs. I couldn't believe that Feelow had put his hands on a woman who loved him like her own. I bent down and put my hands under his arms and told Krystal to grab his feet. Together, we carried him to the back of the truck. Before I got in, I taped his wrists behind his back just in case he woke up before we made it to our destination. That muthafucka had to pay for his violation and I couldn't wait to put my wrath upon him.

****

TAMMY

I watched Marcus and the girl carry Feelow to the back of the truck and put him inside. I didn't have a weapon so I couldn't step out and help Feelow. Marcus taped his ankles and wrists up and then climbed back in the front seat. I started to panic but instead had a better idea. I climbed over to the driver seat of Feelow's car and when Marcus pulled off, I started the car and pulled out so I could follow him. I'll be damned if I let him take Feelow somewhere that he couldn't be found.

I was all Feelow had left to save him. I followed a good distance behind Marcus so he wouldn't notice me. He finally turned off down, a dirt road that led to a big warehouse-like building. I pulled to the side of the road where the vehicle couldn't be seen and watched Marcus and the girl carry Feelow inside. I hoped to save the nigga that had my mind and heart, I just hoped I could make it on time.

Corey Robinson

Chapter Thirteen
MARCUS

When I pulled up to the warehouse, I sat there for a minute without saying anything. Krystal looked at me and asked, "Marcus, are you okay? You know that you can call this off if you want."

I shook my head and then slammed a fist into the dashboard. "Nah, as bad as this is gonna hurt me, it's something I gotta do. I can't keep letting the shit he's been doing go. I've let him get away with it for too long. I wouldn't be able to live with myself, if something had, happened to my mother."

She asked, "Marcus, why did you make me believe that you hated your mother. I didn't even know that ya'll had a relationship. I would like to have gotten to know her."

I let out a long sigh and answered her question. "Our relationship doesn't matter right now okay, and I wasn't ready for you to meet my mother. Nobody, not even those closest to me knew that me and my mother were still talking. I wanted to keep it that way because of shit like this." I stopped talking and looked around and then opened my door and said. "Get out and help me get this nigga in there before he wakes up." I then got out and slammed the door behind me.

Krystal got out a minute later and went to the back of the truck where I was. Together, we lifted Feelow out and carried him inside. When we made it in, I told her., "Drop his feet."At the same time, I let him go and he dropped to the floor with a loud thud.

I pulled a chair up and sat down and waited for him to wake up. Neither Krytal nor I said a word as we waited patiently. After about ten minutes, he finally began to moan. He tried to move his arms but they were still tightly bound behind him. I wasn't about to give him any line of defense. That nigga was going to take the ass whoopin' I had in store for him, because it was one he truly deserved.

I sat and stared, waiting to see how he was going to react to the situation. Krystal stood against the wall and watched me as Feelow finally spoke. "You think you bad, huh, Marcus? This shit with you keeps getting better and better. Ah, look at you now. Your dumb ass still don't remember me, do you?" He grinned wickedly as he stared at Krystal.

I stood up from the chair and kicked Feelow in the stomach and said, "Shut the fuck up, bitch."

His body cringed from the impact and his face turned red as he coughed. He laughed as if the blow had not affected him and said, "What's the matter, Marcus. You don't want her to know that it was me who grabbed her in that alley?" I kicked him again. "Ugh," he moaned.

Krystal came over to where we were.."Marcus, what is he talking about?" she asked.

I answered her question. "Feelow is the nigga that grabbed you in the alley that day. It's just something he does for me when I see women I like. He grabs them and I come behind him and play the hero. But you're the only one I've ever kept. The rest of them, I fucked and sent them on their way. That's why he's so familiar to you."

She looked from me to Feelow and scrunched up her face. "That's some sick shit, Marcus. All this time I felt like I would die for you because you saved me, but that shit was all a plan y'all set up. How the hell do you live with yourself after doing that to women?"

I replied, "Look, it was foul, but look what came out of it."

"Fuck you, Marcus. Don't try to flatter me. It's still bullshit. Just handle your business and let's get the hell outta here. We'll talk about how we met later," she stated with an attitude and went back to stand by the wall.

Fellow laughed. "Nigga, that shit funny as fuck. This shit here is funny too. Yo' weak ass gotta tape a muthafucka's hands and feet up so you can fight him. Soft ass bitch. Had to recruit a white girl to handle your street shit caused you don't know what the fuck you doing."

I kicked Feelow again and let out all my feelings. "Nigga, you were supposed to be my muthafuckin' bro. But somewhere along the way, you went foul. How the fuck could you do me like that, man? We have been doing this shit together since we were kids, Fee. You stabbed me in the back and I still let you slide. I still gave you chances. I stopped other muthafuckas from killing yo' ass and you do what you did to my only girl. You got to pay for that shit, Fee."

I kicked him in the mouth and watched as he spat out blood. He still laughed, and spewed, "Nigga, you had gotten too big for your Dickies. Now, you put that white bitch in my spot like all I have done for you didn't mean shit. You dismissed me like it didn't matter. You didn't even give a fuck about how I felt. I had always been loyal to your fuckin' ass. Nigga, that white bitch has access to the connect. And I don't even know who it is. You've known that bitch for a year, but nigga, I have been there all your life."

I could feel the tears form and decided to let them fall. I wanted Feelow to see just how hurt I really was. As much as I didn't want to, I knew that I would have to kill him. That shit was going to haunt me for the rest of my life but it had to happen. His bad deeds could no longer go unpunished. I walked around his body and said, "Yeah, you were there, Fee but you switched out. You lost your trust in me long ago although I haven't given you a reason. I tried to show you that I was always on your side but you just couldn't figure it out.

"I cut Ditto off because that muthafucka tried you and yet, you still thought I put him on you. I did all I could, Feelow to try and restore our brotherhood, though. I had to be cautious because of the shit you did. This time though, this time, I'm gonna have to end it. You violated my momma nigga. That's shit I can't look over. Fuck everything else. I hope you've made peace with your creator because I'm about to send you to him."

He started to say something else but I stopped him. I kicked him in his face over and over until my shoe was completely covered in blood. Krytal still stood by the wall, her hands covering her mouth at the sight of what she'd witnessed. I finally pulled out my gun and pointed it at his head but before I could put him to sleep for good, my phone rang.

I pulled it out of my pocket and answered, only to hear Keisha's voice, "Marcus! Oh my God! I'm so glad you answered. I'm at the hospital. I had the baby. I want you to come by and see him, he is so damn cute, poor thing looks just like his damn daddy."

I smiled. "Damn girl having that boy is making yo ass talk ninety miles a minute. I'm glad you are okay though sorry about being so hard on you."

Keisha replied, "It's okay, Marcus. I should have listened to you. I knew you was only trying to protect us. I called my cousin but her ass ain't even show up. I haven't called Feelow yet. I think I'll give it a little time before I show my face and let him meet his son."

"Hey, I'll stop by as soon as I'm done handling this business I got going on. Congratulations," I said as she told me the baby's name.

When we hung up, I kneeled down beside Feelow who was barely breathing but still alive and said, "That was Keisha, my nigga. She had the baby. Too bad you'll never meet him but don't worry, I'll take real good care of him for you." I pointed the gun at his head again.

"Wait! Did she tell you his name? At least let me know what his name is before you kill me."

I nodded my head. "Yeah, she told me. His name is Khalif Keyshawn Feeldan," and then, I pulled the trigger.

****

TAMMY

I crept up to the window of the warehouse after Feelow was carried inside and watched them drop him on the floor like he was nothing but trash. I had to put my hand over my mouth to keep myself from screaming. I watched as words were exchanged but could barely hear what was being said. I saw the white girl walk over to Marcus and Feelow and say something but then retreated back to where she stood before.

Marcus started to kick Feelow, first in the stomach and then in the face. I swore that I could feel each kick myself and cringed. The tears formed because I knew that Feelow wasn't going to make it out of there alive and if I was discovered, I wouldn't make it either.

"I'm sorry I can't help you. Oh my God, I'm so sorry," I said to myself. I thought about Keisha and the baby she was at the hospital having all by herself and felt bad. I let a man come in between us. The father of her child. A child that would never meet him. I pulled out my phone to call her and tell her what was happening but decided against it. I didn't want to ruin her happiness with such a tragedy.

I let the tears fall as Marcus put his gun to Feelow's head and then his phone rang. I breathed a sigh of relief and hoped that whoever the caller was, they could stop this from happening instead. When Marcus put his phone back in his pocket, he pointed the gun at Feelow again and said something right before he pulled the trigger.

The girl walked over to Marcus and put her arm to around him as if he was the one who needed comfort. Marcus pulled a knife out of his pocket and bent down to cut the tape off of Feelow's wrists and ankles and put the tape in his pocket. They both took one more look at Feelow and turned around to leave. I tried to get ghost so I wouldn't be seen. I peeped my head up one last time and when I did, I looked the female right in her eyes.

****

KRYSTAL

I could have sworn that I just looked someone in their eyes, so I said to Marcus, "I think I just saw someone looking in the window, Marcus. They looked me dead in the eyes."

He brushed it off and continued to walk back to the truck, saying, "Nah, baby, you just trippin' and shit. Ain't nobody out here but us, and we bout to be muthafucking ghost."

I continued to look around and when I heard Marcus start the truck, I shook my head and jumped in the passenger seat. When I shut the door, Marcus asked me, "How do you feel about what just happened in there. Are you good? You ain't scared or nothing are you?"

I rolled my eyes and replied, "If you're worried about me saying something, don't, I know the drill, Marcus. Did you forget that keeping my mouth shut was part of my training, don't you give yourself any credit for anything you taught me?"

He nodded his head and said, "Yeah, but telling you something and having you there to actually see it is two totally different things. I mean you ain't gonna start having nightmares and shit are you? Wit' your soft ass."

I laughed along with him but deep inside, I was scared as hell. I said, "Shit, if I remember correctly, you were the one shedding tears, I should be asking you if you're alright instead."

He gripped the steering wheel tighter and replied "yeah, that was my brother. It took a lot out of me to do what I just did to him. We were good and then all of a sudden shit just changed. Nigga, must have smoked on some bad shit or something."

I put a hand over his to comfort him and said, "It's alright. You do what you have to do. It's over now so, you can work to move past it. Don't worry, Marcus. I got your back no matter what happens," he raised an eyebrow and stated, "Yeah, I guess we'll find out."

****

TAMMY

When they were gone, I went into the warehouse. "Feelow, Feelow, oh my God, hold on." I lifted his head into my lap and knew that there was nothing I could do to help him. He was gone. "Why didn't I do something, Oh Feelow, I'm so sorry. Please forgive me." I cried out. I couldn't believe that he was dead. What was I going to say to Keishia? This would surely break her heart.

Feelow had always meant the world to me, though I wish that I hadn't said all the shit I'd said to him. I knew that I had to do something to avenge him. Something that would make Marcus pay dearly for his evil deed.

I said to Feelow's lifeless body, "I know, I know what to do. I'm going to make Marcus pay for this shit. I'll avenge you, Feelow. I know just what to do."

I pulled my cell phone out of my pocket and dialed 911. "Hello, this is 911 state your emergency." I was silent for a second but the lady on the other end pulled me back. "Hello, what is your emergency?"

"Yes ... yes. Uhm. I just witnessed a murderer. I watched someone get killed. Please get the muthafucka that did this," I said into the receiver.

"Ma'am, where are you located, who am I talking to and who did you see get murdered?" she asked.

"Feelow. I mean Khalid Feeland. I saw the whole thing. He beat him and then shot him in the head. I saw it all, that bastard killed him," I cried out.

"Alright ma'am. I've got officers on the way to the location showing up on the screen. Do you have the name of the perpetrator?"

"Yes, his name is Marcus Newsome."

****

KEISHA

"Damn, Keisha, that lil nigga looks just like Feelow's ugly ass," Marcus said with a smile.

"Fuck you, Marcus, my son is not ugly. I'm so glad you decided to show up. You wanna hold your nephew?"

Marcus held his arms out for Khalif. I knew that he would be a good uncle to me and Feelow's son. I couldn't wait for Feelow to see our baby and hoped that maybe Little Khalif could bring him and Marcus back together. I wanted both of them in his life so I needed them to let go of their beef and get back right.

I asked him, "Marcus, have you talked to Feelow? I've been calling his phone but he ain't answering and he ain't call back."

He passed Khalif back to me and said somberly, "I'm sorry, Keisha, I thought you knew."

I looked at him curiously. "Knew what? What's going on, Marcus? Is Feelow okay?"

"He's dead, Keisha. They found his body in an old warehouse outside of the city. He had been beaten pretty badly and then shot in the head," Marcus revealed with a painful look in his eyes.

"No, Marcus! Nooo.! What about Khalif? Oh my God, he's never gonna meet his daddy! What am I supposed to tell him when he grows up? Please tell me you're playing a joke, Marcus. Please!" I cried out and held my baby tightly. The thought of my son never knowing his father broke my heart.

"Yeah, that shit got me fucked up too, but I got your back, Keisha," said Marcus, "and this little guy ... we gonna make sure that he knows his daddy was a real muthafucka. We ain't never gonna let Feelow's memory die. I promise I'm gonna keep his spirit alive. I got y'all. Whatever y'all need."

I tried to stop my tears but my heart was broken. "I can't believe he's gone. I shouldn't have ever left him. I'll never be able to get him back. Never!"

About that time, the room door opened and a detective walked in. "Marcus Newsome?" he said.

Marcus replied, "Detective McDonald. How can I help you? Did you find out anything?"

The detective motioned to the officer that was with him and the officer walked over to Marcus and told him to put his hands behind his back. "Marcus Newsome, you are under arrest for the murder of Khalid Keyshawn Feeland. You have the right to remain silent. Anything you say can and will be used against you in the court of law."

I was confused. "Marcus, what's going on? Why are they arresting you for killing Feelow? That can't be right. Marcus, answer me!"

Marcus looked at me.'"This is bullshit, Keisha. Feelow was my brother. Don't worry, I'll be out by the end of the day."

The detective and the officer walked Marcus out of the hospital room and when the door closed, I remembered that Marcus didn't answer my question.

****

KRYSTAL

"So, what do you wanna do?" Trap asked me when I told him that Marcus had been arrested for Feelow's murder.

I replied, "I think that for now, you and Creep need to take over everything so I can keep my mind focused on getting him out of there."

I thought about the eyes that had looked back at me the night Marcus killed Feelow. I wished now that I could have said something. Maybe all of this would have been avoided. I felt like Marcus being arrested was my fault but it was too late to turn back now. "I've contacted the lawyer he told me to contact and he is going to meet with Marcus as we speak. When I leave here I'm going up there to find out what the lawyers are talking about."

"Yo', Krys. When was the last time you heard from Carrie?" Creep asked. "That bitch done got ghost on a nigga."

I had forgotten all about Carrie because I had more important things going on but said," That's a good question, creep. I find it funny that it was her father that arrested Marcus, and that bitch suddenly goes ghost. I'll put feelers out and see if I Can find her. I'll also get with the connect to let him know what's going on. Try to work something out until Marcus can get out of there. Try to do what you can with what I've given you until then."

A sudden knock came at their door and when Trap answered it, Echo and his crew were on the other side. Echo walked in first, and said, "Ay, y'all. I just heard. What can I do to help out the situation?"

"Just keep your ear to the streets. Find out if anyone knows more than what they're telling. I've been informed that there was a witness. I just don't know who it is," I said.

Echo smiled and came closer. "So, you are the snow bunny Marcus had stashed away. Shit, I would've hidden your ass too."

Bossed up, I said, "Step the fuck off. My dude is sitting in a jail cell and you all up on me. I don't get down like that so redirect your bullshit." The room burst out in laughter, although I didn't find a damn thing funny. I turned to Trap and said, "I'll call you as soon as I know something. If you need me before then, you know the number." I walked out to go find out just what the hell I could do to save the man I loved.

****

B-LINE

"The fuck are you doing up here, where is Krys?" I asked Carrie as soon as I opened the door.

She looked spooked. "I called Jambo. He said I could stay for a minute. My father kicked me out because of the company I keep."

"Oh yeah. Daddy the detective. You weren't gonna tell a muthafucka that little bit of information; you ain't think we needed to know that? What's wrong with you?" I pulled her inside roughly.

"Ow, that shit hurts. Jambo told me I could stay. I'm sorry," she cried out.

Jambo walked down the long staircase and walked up on Carrie. He looked at me and nodded and I then asked her, "What do you know about Marcus being arrested on a murder rap by yo' daddy?"

I could tell by the look she gave that she had no clue what we were talking about. She said, "What? I don't know what you're talking about. Marcus was fine when I left. My daddy didn't like me hanging around them but he's a good cop and he would never do no shit like that. My daddy ain't dirty. If he arrested Marcus, then he had a good reason to."

She looked to be telling the truth. I released her from my grasp but threatened, "If I find out anything different, your pops gon be making funeral arrangements so you better be telling the truth." I paused and looked at Jambo. "Get her off the premises. This bitch is going to have to stay far away from here. I don't wanna look at her again until I know for sure she's ignorant to what's happening."

I walked off and went up to my room. I knew that Jambo would take Carrie somewhere safe and where she could be watched. He was really sweet on her so, I knew he'd investigate to make sure she was clean so he could keep her around. I sat down on the edge of my bed and picked up my phone. When I dialed the number, she answered on the first ring.

"What the hell is going on down there? Are you okay?" I asked with concern.

Krystal replied, "I'm fine, Brandon. I'm just trying to do all I can for Marcus. He needs me now more than ever. How did you know something was wrong? I was going to call you."

"I got my sources. People tell me shit when they think it's going to affect me."

"How is Marcus being in jail affecting you? Oh, I'm sorry, that's less money you'll be making, huh Brandon?" she said sarcastically.

I laughed. "Now, you and I both know that his money is mere pocket change to me. His money doesn't mean shit. I'm concerned about you."

"Please don't waste your energy, Brandon. You know I'm not leaving him, especially in a situation like this. What type of person leaves someone when they need them the most? Maybe that's your get down but I'm a real bitch and I won't kick him while he's down. Now, is there something else you need because I'm busy," she said.

I responded and said, "We good but you know you welcome her anytime. What are you going to do if he can't get outta this shit?"

She replied, "Oh, he's gonna get out of it. I give you my word on that. I got him and I'm going to get him out of there. See ya around, Brandon."And then, she hung up in my ear. Her comment threw me off and made me worried. Somehow, I knew in my gut that it would be a long time before I laid eyes on Krystal Madison again. However, no matter how long the wait, I'd be right there with my arms wide open.

Chapter Fourteen
Marcus

"So, what are they talking about?" I asked the attorney.

He looked unhappy with what he was reading but finally answered me. "Well, Mr. Newson, it seems that an eyewitness came forward and said they witnessed you kill Mr. Feeland. Also, I'm seeing they have you as a drug supplier and feel that the murder was drug-related." He lowered his head and looked at me over the rim of his glasses and waited for my response.

"How could there be an eyewitness to something I didn't do? Who the fuck is this witness anyway?"

"Mr. Newsom, there is not any information on who the eyewitness is. However, I see here that they will give a statement but not testify in court. That could work in our favor. I'll do my best to find out the identity but I'm not promising anything," he stated and then closed the file he had sitting in front of him.

"So, what are my chances?" I asked, although I already knew the answer to that question. I was a black man, a thug in the streets, and that alone would make me guilty. I knew that once I got on that stand, it would be over for me and there wasn't shit I could do about it.

He took off his glasses and laid them on the table and leaned back in his chair. "I'm going to keep it straight with you, Mr. Newsome. You're looking at spending the rest of your life inside of prison gates, and honestly, no matter how hard I fight, you're going to serve at least twenty-five mandatory. The victim's wounds were gruesome. He was beaten in the face pretty badly and then, he was shot in the head." He paused and leaned forward and said, "Which means that he was tapped in a manner that kept him from defending himself. You'll be lucky if the state doesn't seek the death penalty. I'm sorry."

I held my head down in the palm of my hands and exclaimed, "Man, I can't sit in prison for the rest of my life. Shit, I can't even do those twenty-five. You gotta do something. This is bullshit, man. What the fuck am I paying you for if you can't make this shit go away? I might as well keep my fucking money. The fuck!"

He shook his head and gathered his files and then put his glasses back on. I watched him walk to the door and I wanted to stop him but I had nothing else to say. He opened the door, then half-turned to look at me. "Perhaps, there was someone else involved. It's either you or them. You decide." Then he walked out.

****

TAMMY

"I'm so sorry I wasn't there for Khalif's birth. I hope you forgive me," I said to Keisha while she sat on the couch and fed her newborn son. It was crazy how much he looked like Feelow and every time I looked at him, my heart broke. I wanted to tell Keisha so badly about what I had seen but I didn't want to cause her any more heartache. One day, she would learn about what happened but until then, I would keep my mouth shut.

She replied, "It's alright cuz, I ain't mad about it anymore. The doctor had me under so much anesthesia that I wouldn't have even known you were there. Shit, I don't think my ass was all the way there," she laughed and then suddenly became quiet. I knew that she was thinking about Feelow. She said, "I just. I just can't believe that he's not here to share in the joy of having this little fella here in our lives. I feel so bad now because I didn't call him. Maybe if I had called, he wouldn't have been in a position for that shit to happen. He would have been with me instead. I know that once he would have laid eyes on Khalif, his life would have been changed forever. I miss him so much."

When she started to cry, I got up and went to sit by her side. The least I could do was comfort her. I hated Marcus but I didn't want her to hate him because of me. If she would have known that I was with Feelow when she called me, she would have been pissed. Marcus was in jail for Feelow's murder and he had convinced Keisha that he didn't touch him and that he was being set up. She believed him, so who was I to tell her anything different.

I put my arm around her and offered her a few comforting words. "Okay, Keisha. I know you miss him but you can keep his memory alive through Khalif. I feel so bad that I almost let some dick come between us. I was being selfish and now, neither one of us has him. I'm sorry."

"It's okay, Tammy, he's probably rolling over in his grave right now because of them blaming Marcus. Those disrespectful muthafuckas arrested him in my hospital room. That is so fucked up. Him and Marcus were like brothers even after all the shit they had gone through. God, I feel so bad for Marcus. Losing his best friend and then getting charged with killing him."

I nodded my head. "Yeah, cuz, I'm feeling you on that. It's a lot to take in. Don't worry though, the truth will come out. You'll see."

"Yeah, and when I find out who really did it, I'm gonna make them pay," Keisha vowed.

I replied, "Somehow cuz, I feel like they're already paying for it."

****

KRYSTAL

I looked at him through the glass and could tell that he had lost all hope. I had never seen Marcus look so defeated, and deep inside I knew that he had given up. Feelow was his best friend and having to take his life was eating Marcus up. I wished that I could carry his pain for him but it was so deep that it would cause me to drown.

"Marcus, what is the lawyer saying? Is he gonna be able to get you outta this mess," I asked.

Marcus looked at me through sleepless eyes and replied, "The fuck you think he is saying? I'm a muthafuckin' black man, Krystal. You know them crackas don't fight for us to be free no matter how much they are being paid. They sit across from you and make you believe that they are fighting for you but they are really working on both sides." He leaned closer to the glass and went on. "See, you ain't gotta worry about this kinda shit. If you were behind this glass for killing a black man, you'd probably be rewarded. But me, nah, they gon throw the muthafuckin' book at my black ass. I don't stand a fuckin' chance."

I sat and listened to his logic and knew that he was right. The justice system wasn't made up to protect the black man. It was made to get rid of them. It had always been that way. I wondered why the witness did not mention me but now, I understood. It would have been useless to put me with a black man committing a crime. The system would swear that I didn't act of my own free will, but they had me fucked up if they thought I would just leave Marcus for dead. I was gonna ride with him no matter how long it took. I was built that way. I was built for *him*.

I thought for a minute and then said, "Marcus, there has to be something we can do. I can't bear the thought of you going to prison for the rest of your life. I mean, I'd be right here holding you down, but I'd rather be able to prevent it." I bit my lip while I thought of some possible remedy. "Maybe we could hire a better lawyer. There's gotta be something."

Marcus looked me up and deep in the eyes before offering, "There's only one thing that could make this shit disappear."

"What is it, Marcus? Tell me. I'll do anything."

And then, he told me his idea.

****

MARCUS

When I told Krystal my idea, she looked at me like I was crazy, but she could tell that I was dead serious. She claimed to be my rider so I needed to know just how far she was willing to ride. There was no way I could continue to sit behind those bars.

I thought about Killisha and felt sick to my stomach. Nobody knew about her, not even Feelow. I kept her tucked away real good because I didn't need her caught up in my shit. I had been fucking Killisha for a little over two years. She was a female I had met before I got into the game. When I didn't have shit, I didn't think I stood a chance with her but no matter how bad I was doing, she was still determined. Those other bitches turned their heads but Killisha smiled at me every time I passed her way. At first, I didn't think I deserved a female like her but she didn't give up. When Ditto pulled me in and made it to where I was getting paper, I finally gave in. I wanted to be able to do stuff for her, although that material shit didn't matter.

She didn't even know that I had been arrested so I figured it would be best if let her know. She was eight months pregnant with my son and I hated to add any stress to her life but I knew that she would get worried. She picked up on the first ring and went off on me. "Really, Marcus? I'm about to have your fucking son in a few weeks and yo' ass is sitting in jail. What the fuck is going on? And your ass better not lie."

"Damn, Killa, give me a fuckin' chance to explain. Your hormones got yo' ass tripping. What the fuck? My ass done got locked up for a murder rap, baby, and all you can do is cuss a nigga out. Chill yo' ass out. You gon stress my fucking' son,"

"A murder rap? How the hell did that happen, Marcus? Who the fuck did you kill?"

"I ain't kill no damn body, but these crackas are trying to hem a nigga up. I just called so you wouldn't worry."

She toned down instantly, and after I explained that I didn't wanna go into details over a recorded phone, she asked, "When can I come to see you?"

"Nah, you stay where you are. I don't need anybody seeing you and coming after you and my seed. Just chill, and don't worry. I got a way to get out of this shit and don't trip when you see me on T.V. I got this."

"So, what am I supposed to do about, Markill? Our son not going to wait to come into this world. When it's his time, he's coming, and I really need you to be there."

"Don't worry, baby. I'll be home before he gets here," I reassured her. The operator came on the line and interrupted our call by telling us that we had thirty seconds left. We said our goodbyes and then hung up.

I sat down and thought about the plan I had to get out of the jail. I hoped that I'd convinced Krystal enough to go along with it.

****

TRAP

The streets had been quiet ever since Marcus got arrested for Feelow's murder. Some mourned the loss and some embraced it and continued with what they were doing. Of course, the fiends had no clue of anything, as long as they could continue getting high, they were fine with whatever else was going on. Marcus had said something about an eyewitness, but I couldn't find out who it was. As for Krystal, she seemed to be in her own world, trying to figure out how to get Marcus out of his situation.

"Yo dawg, are you good over there? What you thinking about?" I asked Creep, as he sat at the table with a handful of money. He was staring off into space so I knew his mind was elsewhere.

Creep finally looked up and replied, "Man, I can't believe we can't find that bitch Carrie. That shit makes me feel like something up, but I'm telling you that if I find out she had a hand in this shit with Marcus, I will kill that bitch while her fuckin' pig ass daddy watches, and if them muthafuckin' mutts wanna get down, they can get the dealt with too."

"Yeah, Creep a nigga feel you on that shit. It's mighty funny that bitch told her fuck ass daddy that she wasn't leaving thug niggas alone and then this happens! that's why called to apologize for anything. I snuck wanna kill that bitch on G.P," I stated.

Creep chuckled. He came and sat down in the chair across from me. "Man, I know Marcus is feeling kinda empty about this shit with Fee. What do you think gonna happen to our boy?"

I answered honestly, "Dawg, them crackas gon throw the book at him if they get the chance, and ain't shit we can do if they have an eyewitness. It's kinda funny the feinds ain't talking about it. Krys said Marcus is shook about all this."

"Bro, I have seen Marcus be a lot of things but I ain't never seen his black ass scared," said Creep. The room fell silent until a few minutes later when Creep's phone rang. "Yo," he answered. After a few minutes, he hung up, looked at me and said, "I found Carrie."

I sat up quickly. "What? Man, where the fuck is she?'

Creep shook his head and his nose flared as he responded, "With the connect?"

****

KEISHA

The days passed by slowly and each day was harder than the last. I had taken Khalif to the jail to see Marcus. I know he was hurting from Feelow's passing but I'd hoped that having Fee's son in his life would make it easier for him to do the time until they found out the truth and released him.

I asked, "Marcus, how're you holding up in here? Is there anything I can do?"

He shook his head and said, Nah, Keisha, ain't much anyone can do until they get the person who really did it. I just can't believe that my nigga is really gone. I mean we have been through a lot of shit but damn, I wouldn't ever take my brother out like that. He was my fucking heart."

"I know, Marcus, and I wish I could do something," I said.

He replied, "Just keep coming to check in on a nigga, Keisha. That's about all you can do right now. Keep bringing lil man up here so he won't ever forget my face." He leaned closer to the glass that divided us and said, "I'm about to tell you some shit that nobody else in the entire world knows but I need to know that I can trust you."

I reached over and laid Khalif in his baby carrier and leaned in closer to the glass, speaking quietly. "Marcus, you can trust me with anything. I mean, I know I messed up when I dipped on you and went to Feelow but I was just following my heart. I truly loved him."

"Yeah, I know," he replied. "Look, I have a girl whose name is Killisha. She has been wit' me even before all the cheddar and shit. Lil mama is real as fuck. She's carrying my seed right now, and she is gonna have him soon. I'm hoping to be outta here before he comes but just in case I'm not, I need you to be there."

I was shocked at what I'd just heard but I quickly agreed. "Um, yeah, Marcus. Okay, I got you, but how did you hide her for all this time and nobody knew about her? I mean, you're about to be a whole daddy. Damn, Marcus, I'm so happy for you. Shit, you gotta get outta here."

"Yeah, that's what I've been hollering. But look, Keisha I'm gonna give you shawty's number and I want y'all to meet up. I want Feelow's son and my son to grow up together. I'd like them to carry on me and my boy's legacy together. Give me your word that you'll look out for them until I get out this bitch."

I said, "I give you my word, Marcus. Together, we gonna make you and Feelow stay alive forever. Don't worry about a thing." I smiled, but deep inside I couldn't wait to meet the bitch that held my spot on the throne.

****

CARRIE

I had my ear to the door and listened while B-Line talked to Jambo, "Yo, dawg, her ass can't stay up in my shit. So you need to find someplace else for her to go."

"Ah come on, B. I'm feeling lil mama. I need her to be around all the time," Jambo said.

B-Line replied, "Well, you can keep her around all the time when you get y'all a place. She ain't staying here! I'm sorry, bro, something ain't right 'bout that crazy-ass girl, and her fucking daddy ain't gonna be running up in my shit."

"What's up with you, man? You mad 'cause that other bitch ain't come with her?"

I heard a little tussle and then, B-line said, "Get that bitch and get the fuck outta my shit. Don't make me question your loyalty"

"Aiight. I just need a couple of days to get us a place. My bad, homie, I was tripping," Jambo said right before I heard footsteps.

I hurriedly ran back downstairs and went to sit at the bar in the kitchen. I turned on the small television set and then got out a snack and prepared to watch Real Housewives of Atlanta. A couple of minutes passed and then, I heard a phone ring. I looked around and noticed the cell phone sitting beside the microwave. I got up so I could get close to the phone and when I saw who the caller was, I picked up. "Hello?"

The person on the other end didn't say anything. Click! They hung up.

****

KRYSTAL

I had thought about what Marcus asked me to do and wasn't sure if I would be able to go through with it. I had sacrificed so much for him in such a short time. Did I have the strength to sacrifice anymore? I asked myself.

I'd had no one but him and wondered just what I'd do if he went away for the rest of his life. How could this have happened? I kept reliving the scene, which made it hard to sleep. Somehow, I felt like Feelow was going to come back and get me the same way he'd gotten me in that alley.

The knock on the car window broke me from my thoughts and I looked up to see Trap standing there as he stared at me with concerned eyes. I got out and said, "Hey, Trap. I'm sorry I was just thinking about Marcus and all the bullshit going on."

Trap replied, "You good, I was just checking on you. I heard you pull up but when you never came to the door, I figured I'd come out. Guess I don't need to ask you how you're holding up."

Corey Robinson

I flashed a fake smile. "I'm not doing too great right now. The people are talking twenty-five to life if Marcus is found guilty. I'm not sure I can live with that."

He folded his arms across his chest and leaned against the car. "Yeah, Krys, that's a long-ass time for a nigga like Marcus to sit up behind those walls. That nigga had always stood tall for Feelow no matter what that muthafucka did. Nigga is loyal as fuck and I just don't see him going out and knocking him off like that. Shit don't seem right."

I looked up at him and asked, "Why y'all are so damn worried about me? The question is: how are you and Creep holding up? Y'all 'bout the only ones he has left."

"Yeah, that's my peoples. Bro, ain't never did me dirty. Even when Feelow tried to convince him that I was short on the cheddar, that nigga defended us. He knew we'd never pull no shit like that. If he would have been a lesser nigga, he would have come over here and put lead in both our skulls. I miss his black ass." Trap shook his head in despair. "Yo, you wanna come inside and chill for a minute?"

"Nah, Trap. There's something I need to take care of. I just wanted to come and check on y'all. I'll keep y'all up on what I can until I see y'all again."

Trap bent down and gave me a hug. "Keep ya head up. If you ever need us don't hesitate to make that call. I got everything under control so you just keep your focus on Marcus and help get him outta there."

I smiled and got in my car to leave. Trap stood there until I pulled out of the driveway. Marcus needed good people like him in his life. I drove to the home that Marcus and I had shared and tried to focus but my mind would only let me think of Marcus. I felt guilty about him being in jail, and knew that I had to make a decision quickly. His trial would start in two days and deep down, I knew that I was the only one that could save him.

I drew a hot bath and relaxed so I could ease the aching feeling in my stomach. I needed to make a decision and I needed to do

174

it soon. I was confused. There was only one thing that would help me make up my mind.

I got out of the tub and put my robe without drying off. I sat on the edge of the bed that Marcus and I had shared and picked up the phone. Slowly, I dialed the number that I had held in my mind and heart. A number I had never dialed before.

I listened while the phone rang several times and right when I was about to give up, someone answered, "Hello." I sat there for a minute and took in the voice. "Hello?" A tear formed in my eyes as I pulled the phone away. I then hit the end button and made my decision.

****

KRYSTAL

The day of Marcus' trial had finally arrived. I got up earlier than usual so that I could prepare myself for what I needed to do. Marcus had been there for me from day one and now, it was time for me to return the favor. I thought about the phone call I had made and it broke my heart. "How could you?" I asked out loud, but knew that I was wrong. Who was I to be mad about someone else when all along I had someone else myself. She had every right to be where she was, so now I had lost out both ways.

I walked around the room where Marcus had made love to me one more time. I could still feel his pleasure and the scent of his body on top of me. A luxury I wouldn't have for a long time.

I thought about Trap and Creep. I knew that everything I had given to them would be in good hands until Marcus could get back at 'em. I wiped the tear that ran down my cheek and looked around one last time. "God, I'm gonna miss you, Marcus," I said to myself.

I wrote a short note and stuck it on the refrigerator so when Marcus finally made it home, he would see it. He would know just what he meant to me but I didn't want him to feel bad about anything. The weight of killing his best friend was already on his shoulders.

I finally walked out and called an Uber to take me to my final destination. One that had me nervous as hell, but I needed to be there. That was my chance to prove that all Marcus had taught me was well worth it.

The driver pulled up to where I asked him to take me. When I got out of the backseat, my heart beat fast. To say that I was scared as hell would be an understatement. *Come on, Krys. You gotta do this.* I proceeded up the steps. The closer I got to where I needed to be the further away it seemed. I finally made it to the door. *Okay, here it goes.* Determinedly, I walked into reality.

****

MARCUS

"Where the fuck are you? I'm a cuss her ass out when I see her," I said and gripped the bars tighter. I had been calling Krystal all morning and she never answered. I wanted to think the worst but I felt in my heart that she hadn't left me for dead.

"Newsome, it's time. They're ready for you," the bailiff stated as he unlocked the holding cell and placed the cuffs on me.

"Is this shit called for?" I said.

He looked at me funny but never answered the question. Instead, he grabbed me by the arm and pulled me from the cell. The sound of my heartbeat drowned out all other noise. I was nervous as fuck.

When we walked into the courtroom, I looked around. When I laid eyes on Killisha, I smiled while my stomach turned flips. I looked for Krystal but her ass was nowhere in sight.

I saw Trap and nodded my head and he returned the gesture. I knew Creep wouldn't show because he felt that it would be a bad omen.

The opening statements were made from both sides. The picture the prosecution painted made me look like a beast but I was far from that.

As the trial proceeded and witnesses had been questioned and cross-examined, I was shocked when they asked me to take the stand on my own behalf. But I did what I had to do.

The prosecutor asked, "Mr. Newsome, where were you on the night of September twelfth?" The room was eerily quiet as they awaited my answer but before I got a chance to get one word out, the doors to the courtroom opened and the one person who could change it all walked in...

Corey Robinson

Chapter Fifteen
KRYSTAL

My eyes wouldn't open no matter how hard I tried to make them, but I could faintly hear voices in the background.

The cut was pretty deep and she's lost a lot of blood. She's lucky to be alive.

I didn't recognize the male voice but if he knew the truth about me, he wouldn't think that I was so lucky after all. I didn't have shit to live for and was pissed at them for not letting me die. The room went silent for a few seconds and then, I heard the familiar voice of the officer that had alerted them to my deadly sin.

I just don't understand why she would do this when she's scheduled to be released next week after ten straight years.

If only they would have known that by saving my life, they had put someone else's in jeopardy. I wanted to payback more than ever. Marcus deserved to suffer and I wouldn't stop until he did.

When the voices finally faded slowly in the distance, I laid there and plotted my revenge because hell hath no fury like a woman scorned.

To Be Continued…
Protégé of a Legend 3
Coming Soon

Corey Robinson

Lock Down Publications and Ca$h Presents assisted publishing packages.

BASIC PACKAGE $499

Editing

Cover Design

Formatting

UPGRADED PACKAGE $800

Typing

Editing

Cover Design

Formatting

ADVANCE PACKAGE $1,200

Typing

Editing

Cover Design

Formatting

Copyright registration

Proofreading

Upload book to Amazon

LDP SUPREME PACKAGE $1,500

Typing

Editing

Protégé of a Legend 2

Cover Design

Formatting

Copyright registration

Proofreading

Set up Amazon account

Upload book to Amazon

Advertise on LDP Amazon and Facebook page

***Other services available upon request. Additional charges may apply

Lock Down Publications

P.O. Box 944

Stockbridge, GA 30281-9998

Phone # 470 303-9761

Submission Guideline

Submit the first three chapters of your completed manuscript to ldpsubmissions@gmail.com, subject line: Your book's title. The manuscript must be in a .doc file and sent as an attachment. Document should be in Times New Roman, double spaced and in size 12 font. Also, provide your synopsis and full contact information. If sending multiple submissions, they must each be in a separate email.

Have a story but no way to send it electronically? You can still submit to LDP/Ca$h Presents. Send in the first three chapters, written or typed, of your completed manuscript to:

LDP: Submissions Dept
Po Box 944
Stockbridge, Ga 30281

DO NOT send original manuscript. Must be a duplicate.

Provide your synopsis and a cover letter containing your full contact information.

Thanks for considering LDP and Ca$h Presents.

NEW RELEASES

THE COCAINE PRINCESS 6 by KING RIO

VICIOUS LOYALTY 3 by KINGPEN

SOUL OF A HUSTLER, HEART OF A KILLER 2 by SAYNOMORE

SOSA GANG by ROMELL TUKES

PROTÉGÉ OF A LEGEND 2 by COREY ROBINSON

Corey Robinson

STRAIGHT BEAST MODE III
De'Kari
KINGPIN KILLAZ IV
STREET KINGS III
PAID IN BLOOD III
CARTEL KILLAZ IV
DOPE GODS III
Hood Rich
SINS OF A HUSTLA II
ASAD
YAYO V
Bred In The Game 2
S. Allen
THE STREETS WILL TALK II
By Yolanda Moore
SON OF A DOPE FIEND III
HEAVEN GOT A GHETTO II
SKI MASK MONEY II
By Renta
LOYALTY AIN'T PROMISED III
By Keith Williams
I'M NOTHING WITHOUT HIS LOVE II
SINS OF A THUG II
TO THE THUG I LOVED BEFORE II
IN A HUSTLER I TRUST II
By Monet Dragun
QUIET MONEY IV
EXTENDED CLIP III
THUG LIFE IV
By **Trai'Quan**

Corey Robinson

THE STREETS MADE ME IV
By **Larry D. Wright**
IF YOU CROSS ME ONCE III
ANGEL V
By **Anthony Fields**
THE STREETS WILL NEVER CLOSE IV
By **K'ajji**
HARD AND RUTHLESS III
KILLA KOUNTY IV
By **Khufu**
MONEY GAME III
By **Smoove Dolla**
JACK BOYS VS DOPE BOYS IV
A GANGSTA'S QUR'AN V
COKE GIRLZ II
COKE BOYS II
LIFE OF A SAVAGE V
CHI'RAQ GANGSTAS V
SOSA GANG II
By **Romell Tukes**
MURDA WAS THE CASE III
Elijah R. Freeman
THE STREETS NEVER LET GO III
By **Robert Baptiste**
AN UNFORESEEN LOVE IV
BABY, I'M WINTERTIME COLD III
By **Meesha**

QUEEN OF THE ZOO III
By **Black Migo**

A GANGSTA'S PAIN III
By J-Blunt
CONFESSIONS OF A JACKBOY III
By Nicholas Lock
GRIMEY WAYS III
By Ray Vinci
KING KILLA II
By Vincent "Vitto" Holloway
BETRAYAL OF A THUG III
By Fre$h
THE MURDER QUEENS III
By Michael Gallon
THE BIRTH OF A GANGSTER III
By Delmont Player
TREAL LOVE II
By Le'Monica Jackson
FOR THE LOVE OF BLOOD III
By Jamel Mitchell
RAN OFF ON DA PLUG II
By Paper Boi Rari
HOOD CONSIGLIERE III
By Keese
PRETTY GIRLS DO NASTY THINGS II
By Nicole Goosby
PROTÉGÉ OF A LEGEND III
By Corey Robinson
IT'S JUST ME AND YOU II
By Ah'Million
BORN IN THE GRAVE III
By Self Made Tay

Corey Robinson

FOREVER GANGSTA III
By Adrian Dulan
GORILLAZ IN THE TRENCHES II
By SayNoMore
THE COCAINE PRINCESS VII
By King Rio
CRIME BOSS II
Playa Ray
LOYALTY IS EVERYTHING III
Molotti
HERE TODAY GONE TOMORROW II
By Fly Rock
REAL G'S MOVE IN SILENCE II
By Von Diesel

Available Now

RESTRAINING ORDER **I & II**
By **CA$H & Coffee**
LOVE KNOWS NO BOUNDARIES **I II & III**
By **Coffee**
RAISED AS A GOON I, II, III & IV
BRED BY THE SLUMS I, II, III
BLAST FOR ME I & II
ROTTEN TO THE CORE I II III
A BRONX TALE I, II, III
DUFFLE BAG CARTEL I II III IV V VI

188

HEARTLESS GOON I II III IV V
A SAVAGE DOPEBOY I II
DRUG LORDS I II III
CUTTHROAT MAFIA I II
KING OF THE TRENCHES
By **Ghost**
LAY IT DOWN **I & II**
LAST OF A DYING BREED I II
BLOOD STAINS OF A SHOTTA I & II III
By **Jamaica**
LOYAL TO THE GAME I II III
LIFE OF SIN I, II III
By **TJ & Jelissa**
BLOODY COMMAS I & II
SKI MASK CARTEL I II & III
KING OF NEW YORK I II,III IV V
RISE TO POWER I II III
COKE KINGS I II III IV V
BORN HEARTLESS I II III IV
KING OF THE TRAP I II
By **T.J. Edwards**
IF LOVING HIM IS WRONG...I & II
LOVE ME EVEN WHEN IT HURTS I II III
By **Jelissa**
WHEN THE STREETS CLAP BACK I & II III
THE HEART OF A SAVAGE I II III IV
MONEY MAFIA I II
LOYAL TO THE SOIL I II III
By **Jibril Williams**
A DISTINGUISHED THUG STOLE MY HEART I II & III

Corey Robinson

LOVE SHOULDN'T HURT I II III IV

RENEGADE BOYS I II III IV

PAID IN KARMA I II III

SAVAGE STORMS I II III

AN UNFORESEEN LOVE I II III

BABY, I'M WINTERTIME COLD I II

By **Meesha**

A GANGSTER'S CODE I &, II III

A GANGSTER'S SYN I II III

THE SAVAGE LIFE I II III

CHAINED TO THE STREETS I II III

BLOOD ON THE MONEY I II III

A GANGSTA'S PAIN I II

By J-Blunt

PUSH IT TO THE LIMIT

By **Bre' Hayes**

BLOOD OF A BOSS **I, II, III, IV, V**

SHADOWS OF THE GAME

TRAP BASTARD

By **Askari**

THE STREETS BLEED MURDER **I, II & III**

THE HEART OF A GANGSTA I II& III

By **Jerry Jackson**

CUM FOR ME I II III IV V VI VII VIII

An **LDP Erotica Collaboration**

BRIDE OF A HUSTLA **I II & II**

THE FETTI GIRLS **I, II& III**

CORRUPTED BY A GANGSTA I, II III, IV

BLINDED BY HIS LOVE

THE PRICE YOU PAY FOR LOVE I, II ,III

Protégé of a Legend 2

DOPE GIRL MAGIC I II III

By **Destiny Skai**

WHEN A GOOD GIRL GOES BAD

By **Adrienne**

THE COST OF LOYALTY I II III

By Kweli

A GANGSTER'S REVENGE **I II III & IV**

THE BOSS MAN'S DAUGHTERS I II III IV V

A SAVAGE LOVE **I & II**

BAE BELONGS TO ME I II

A HUSTLER'S DECEIT I, II, III

WHAT BAD BITCHES DO I, II, III

SOUL OF A MONSTER I II III

KILL ZONE

A DOPE BOY'S QUEEN I II III

TIL DEATH

By **Aryanna**

A KINGPIN'S AMBITON

A KINGPIN'S AMBITION **II**

I MURDER FOR THE DOUGH

By **Ambitious**

TRUE SAVAGE I II III IV V VI VII

DOPE BOY MAGIC I, II, III

MIDNIGHT CARTEL I II III

CITY OF KINGZ I II

NIGHTMARE ON SILENT AVE

THE PLUG OF LIL MEXICO II

CLASSIC CITY

By **Chris Green**

A DOPEBOY'S PRAYER

Corey Robinson

By **Eddie "Wolf" Lee**
THE KING CARTEL **I, II & III**
By **Frank Gresham**
THESE NIGGAS AIN'T LOYAL **I, II & III**
By **Nikki Tee**
GANGSTA SHYT **I II &III**
By **CATO**
THE ULTIMATE BETRAYAL
By **Phoenix**
BOSS'N UP **I , II & III**
By **Royal Nicole**
I LOVE YOU TO DEATH
By **Destiny J**
I RIDE FOR MY HITTA
I STILL RIDE FOR MY HITTA
By **Misty Holt**
LOVE & CHASIN' PAPER
By **Qay Crockett**
TO DIE IN VAIN
SINS OF A HUSTLA
By **ASAD**
BROOKLYN HUSTLAZ
By **Boogsy Morina**
BROOKLYN ON LOCK I & II
By **Sonovia**
GANGSTA CITY
By **Teddy Duke**
A DRUG KING AND HIS DIAMOND I & II III
A DOPEMAN'S RICHES
HER MAN, MINE'S TOO I, II

192

Protégé of a Legend 2

CASH MONEY HO'S

THE WIFEY I USED TO BE I II

PRETTY GIRLS DO NASTY THINGS

By Nicole Goosby

TRAPHOUSE KING **I II & III**

KINGPIN KILLAZ I II III

STREET KINGS I II

PAID IN BLOOD **I II**

CARTEL KILLAZ I II III

DOPE GODS I II

By **Hood Rich**

LIPSTICK KILLAH **I, II, III**

CRIME OF PASSION I II & III

FRIEND OR FOE I II III

By **Mimi**

STEADY MOBBN' **I, II, III**

THE STREETS STAINED MY SOUL I II III

By **Marcellus Allen**

WHO SHOT YA **I, II, III**

SON OF A DOPE FIEND I II

HEAVEN GOT A GHETTO

SKI MASK MONEY

Renta

GORILLAZ IN THE BAY **I II III IV**

TEARS OF A GANGSTA I II

3X KRAZY I II

STRAIGHT BEAST MODE I II

DE'KARI

TRIGGADALE I II III

MURDAROBER WAS THE CASE I II

Corey Robinson

Elijah R. Freeman
GOD BLESS THE TRAPPERS I, II, III
THESE SCANDALOUS STREETS I, II, III
FEAR MY GANGSTA I, II, III IV, V
THESE STREETS DON'T LOVE NOBODY I, II
BURY ME A G I, II, III, IV, V
A GANGSTA'S EMPIRE I, II, III, IV
THE DOPEMAN'S BODYGAURD I II
THE REALEST KILLAZ I II III
THE LAST OF THE OGS I II III

Tranay Adams
THE STREETS ARE CALLING

Duquie Wilson
MARRIED TO A BOSS I II III

By Destiny Skai & Chris Green
KINGZ OF THE GAME I II III IV V VI
CRIME BOSS

Playa Ray
SLAUGHTER GANG I II III
RUTHLESS HEART I II III

By Willie Slaughter
FUK SHYT

By Blakk Diamond
DON'T F#CK WITH MY HEART I II

By Linnea
ADDICTED TO THE DRAMA I II III
IN THE ARM OF HIS BOSS II

By Jamila
YAYO I II III IV
A SHOOTER'S AMBITION I II

194

BRED IN THE GAME
By S. Allen
TRAP GOD I II III
RICH $AVAGE I II III
MONEY IN THE GRAVE I II III
By Martell Troublesome Bolden
FOREVER GANGSTA I II
GLOCKS ON SATIN SHEETS I II
By Adrian Dulan
TOE TAGZ I II III IV
LEVELS TO THIS SHYT I II
IT'S JUST ME AND YOU
By Ah'Million
KINGPIN DREAMS I II III
RAN OFF ON DA PLUG
By Paper Boi Rari
CONFESSIONS OF A GANGSTA I II III IV
CONFESSIONS OF A JACKBOY I II
By Nicholas Lock
I'M NOTHING WITHOUT HIS LOVE
SINS OF A THUG
TO THE THUG I LOVED BEFORE
A GANGSTA SAVED XMAS
IN A HUSTLER I TRUST
By Monet Dragun
CAUGHT UP IN THE LIFE I II III
THE STREETS NEVER LET GO I II
By Robert Baptiste
NEW TO THE GAME I II III
MONEY, MURDER & MEMORIES I II III

Corey Robinson

By **Malik D. Rice**
LIFE OF A SAVAGE I II III IV
A GANGSTA'S QUR'AN I II III IV
MURDA SEASON I II III
GANGLAND CARTEL I II III
CHI'RAQ GANGSTAS I II III IV
KILLERS ON ELM STREET I II III
JACK BOYZ N DA BRONX I II III
A DOPEBOY'S DREAM I II III
JACK BOYS VS DOPE BOYS I II III
COKE GIRLZ
COKE BOYS
SOSA GANG
By **Romell Tukes**
LOYALTY AIN'T PROMISED I II
By **Keith Williams**
QUIET MONEY I II III
THUG LIFE I II III
EXTENDED CLIP I II
A GANGSTA'S PARADISE
By **Trai'Quan**
THE STREETS MADE ME I II III
By **Larry D. Wright**
THE ULTIMATE SACRIFICE I, II, III, IV, V, VI
KHADIFI
IF YOU CROSS ME ONCE I II
ANGEL I II III IV
IN THE BLINK OF AN EYE
By **Anthony Fields**
THE LIFE OF A HOOD STAR

Protégé of a Legend 2

By Ca$h & Rashia Wilson
THE STREETS WILL NEVER CLOSE I II III
By K'ajji
CREAM I II III
THE STREETS WILL TALK
By Yolanda Moore
NIGHTMARES OF A HUSTLA I II III
By King Dream
CONCRETE KILLA I II III
VICIOUS LOYALTY I II III
By Kingpen
HARD AND RUTHLESS I II
MOB TOWN 251
THE BILLIONAIRE BENTLEYS I II III
REAL G'S MOVE IN SILENCE
By Von Diesel
GHOST MOB
Stilloan Robinson
MOB TIES I II III IV V VI
SOUL OF A HUSTLER, HEART OF A KILLER I II
GORILLAZ IN THE TRENCHES
By SayNoMore
BODYMORE MURDERLAND I II III
THE BIRTH OF A GANGSTER I II
By Delmont Player
FOR THE LOVE OF A BOSS
By C. D. Blue
MOBBED UP I II III IV
THE BRICK MAN I II III IV V
THE COCAINE PRINCESS I II III IV V VI

197

Corey Robinson

By King Rio

KILLA KOUNTY I II III IV

By Khufu

MONEY GAME I II

By Smoove Dolla

A GANGSTA'S KARMA I II III

By FLAME

KING OF THE TRENCHES I II III

by **GHOST & TRANAY ADAMS**

QUEEN OF THE ZOO I II

By **Black Migo**

GRIMEY WAYS I II

By Ray Vinci

XMAS WITH AN ATL SHOOTER

By Ca$h & Destiny Skai

KING KILLA

By Vincent "Vitto" Holloway

BETRAYAL OF A THUG I II

By Fre$h

THE MURDER QUEENS I II

By Michael Gallon

TREAL LOVE

By Le'Monica Jackson

FOR THE LOVE OF BLOOD I II

By Jamel Mitchell

HOOD CONSIGLIERE I II

By Keese

PROTÉGÉ OF A LEGEND I II

By Corey Robinson

BORN IN THE GRAVE I II

Protégé of a Legend 2

By Self Made Tay

MOAN IN MY MOUTH

By XTASY

TORN BETWEEN A GANGSTER AND A GENTLEMAN

By J-BLUNT & Miss Kim

LOYALTY IS EVERYTHING I II

Molotti

HERE TODAY GONE TOMORROW

By Fly Rock

PILLOW PRINCESS

By S. Hawkins

BOOKS BY LDP'S CEO, CA$H

TRUST IN NO MAN

TRUST IN NO MAN 2

TRUST IN NO MAN 3

BONDED BY BLOOD

SHORTY GOT A THUG

THUGS CRY

THUGS CRY 2

THUGS CRY 3

TRUST NO BITCH

TRUST NO BITCH 2

TRUST NO BITCH 3

TIL MY CASKET DROPS

RESTRAINING ORDER

RESTRAINING ORDER 2

IN LOVE WITH A CONVICT

LIFE OF A HOOD STAR

XMAS WITH AN ATL SHOOTER

Protégé of a Legend 2

CPSIA information can be obtained
at www.ICGtesting.com
Printed in the USA
LVHW041836240223
740361LV00001B/117

9 781958 111796